HEAVENLY

BY THOMAS DUFFY

Copyright 2021 Thomas Duffy

ISBN-13: 9798718984675

Cover Design

Erica Velasco

Heavenly by Thomas Duffy

Chapter One

A man always wonders about the purpose of his life. It was a late night/early morning. The date was June 18th, 2019. John Robinson, 43-years old, was walking on the subway platform at Times Square station at 1:15 AM. Dodging some homeless people asking for money along the way, he paced back and forth as he waited for a number 7 train to take him to his apartment in Queens. He was coming from his late-night shift working at a movie theater.

John loved films. Movies gave him the desire to live and pursue his job fruitfully. He liked happy endings in modern cinema although, most of the time in his life, he was far from reaching a traditional happy ending of his own. He had no children and was never married. His longest relationship with a female was nineteen months. He had personal ads on every dating site imaginable from Match.com to Plenty of Fish.

With receding brown hair and brown eyes, John stood at 5'10" and weighed 197 lbs. John would probably not be deemed the worst find on a dating site nor would he be considered the best. When considering his salary at his job, he resided somewhere near the bottom of the batch of ads posted on these sites. However, John loved what he did. Interacting with customers and discussing movies with them made him happy.

Religion was something that John seemed to have let go of after college. He had lost both parents at a fairly young age and had one sibling who was now married with children. It was a sister whose name was Meredith and she lived on the West Coast in California. They were both born in Queens, New York in the late 1970's. Meredith still practiced Catholicism while John was too busy sleeping on

Sunday mornings recovering from his late Saturday nights working at the movie theater.

When John finally boarded the 7 train, he managed to get a seat and fell into a light sleep until he got to his stop a half hour later. John's body had become so accustomed to this kind of nap after work ended but he, somehow, always managed to get off at the right stop to catch the connecting train that would take him to his studio apartment.

Upon his arrival home, he poured himself a nice cup of soda over five cubes of ice. Even though the soda had caffeine, he was so tired that, after drinking it, he fell into a deep sleep. His dream period consisted of taunting visions of happiness that were so far from reality that, when he woke up the next day, he didn't have to think much in order to figure out what was real and what was not.

A few messages were in his mailboxes on the dating sites that he was signed up with. Unfortunately, the news was not good in terms of the answers he received from the women whose ads he had replied to.

His cell phone started to ring. John noticed the 1-800 number to be that of a creditor who he owed money to. John proceeded not to answer the call. His money had to be directed towards the more urgent expenses he had to pay that month— namely, the rent for his apartment.

Chapter Two

John was at work cleaning the concession stand later that evening. He was working with a recent hire. She was a Jewish woman in her late 20's named Mina who was helping him by stocking the candy under the register for the customers to see.

"So, Brad Pitt has a new movie coming out this summer," John informed her.

"I don't watch the movies," Mina replied.

"Why do you work here if you don't like the movies?"

"My husband told me they were hiring. I needed a job."

"I see," John said realizing that not every employee would share his passion for the cinema.

A 32-year old Hispanic man named Jose was the general manager of the theater. He called John over to discuss his work performance during the downtime between showings of the movies which were playing there.

"You're always on time, and you work hard," Jose informed him.

"Thanks for noticing that."

"You're welcome. However, I had a customer call me a couple weeks ago who said you overcharged her on a large popcorn and large soda."

"Impossible. The price comes up on the screen."

"That's true but she said you must have done something incorrectly. This is because the point-of-sale system did not apply the proper discount accordingly. She said she had added a box of Goobers to the order as well. Did you tell her the whole order would be cheaper if she added a candy?"

"I told her that it was the best deal not the cheapest deal."

"Just be careful. It is just the little things like this which keep on happening, unfortunately. They hold you back from advancing to a better position with the company."

"I made the theater money, didn't I?"

"I had to refund this whole order for this lady. We lost money on the deal."

"I understand. I'll be more careful in the future."

John was frustrated the rest of the night realizing that, every time he thought he was close to doing well in advancing with the company, something would happen to take him two steps back. He remained friendly to the guests at the theater that night. He kept some positivity within himself. It didn't matter how hopeless he felt after Jose's feedback. He wanted to move forward and do better. On to the subway platform that night, after work, John saw an oversized rat had made its way. John kept his distance as he paced back and forth continuing to wait for his 7 train to come. The rat made him feel uneasy but having lived in New York all his life, he was used to such happenings.

John had not reached out to his sister, Meredith, recently. He wanted to call her to see how she and her family were doing. It never occurred to him that she may have welcomed such a call with open arms. Instead, he always thought about the conflicting hours of their jobs and thought, for whatever reason, that she may reject his phone call.

John slept well the next few nights continuing to live his lonely existence. In an interesting dream one night, he caught a glimpse of what seemed to be Jesus Christ, himself. John was back in church as a young boy making his Holy Eucharist. Jesus distributed the communion to him in the vision. John also felt nervous being in front of Jesus in the dream. He didn't know why he felt that way. It remained quite interesting to John that he conjured up such an interesting scenario and felt that maybe the dream symbolized his need to go back to church again.

Chapter Three

It was a few days later when John got up one early afternoon to go to work. All his important bills were up to date. John felt accomplished. As he walked to the train station, he felt sadness that he could not have found anyone interesting to date recently. It seemed his age was a major problem. He wasn't young enough to meet women who had no personal baggage. Everyone he dated seemed to have been married or had children from a previous relationship. Although he, himself, had what he would call emotional baggage, he had no serious romantic history to speak of nor did he have any children.

It was a Saturday evening at around 4 in the afternoon when John found himself getting off the train and walking through a tunnel at Times Square train station. There were flickering lights over his head as he started to hear noise. There was indistinct loud yelling and screaming. Police were apparently trying to apprehend someone. One police officer had a young male pinned to the ground while other cops were approaching the scene. The suspect had a gun in his hand while other people in the station were trying to flee the scene.

John started to turn around to run away as the guy shot his gun before an officer removed it from his hands. The bullet from the gun hit John from behind as he fell to the ground. John felt pain in his stomach and closed his eyes. A bright light started shining. That white light was all John could see as he no longer felt himself attached to his body.

John began to feel a rush as he saw a tunnel moving quite fast. He seemed to be moving along the tunnel in an inexplicable way. Then, he felt himself back in his body. He had no clothes on as he found himself walking on a cloud. He heard a voice scream, "Jump on to the next cloud!"

As the long cloud he was walking naked on started nearing its end, John jumped to the next cloud when he heard the male voice he heard previously scream, "Keep jumping on the clouds, John!"

After jumping on to three different clouds, there was a platform. He stepped on to it. There were two lines of people, all naked males. Some were old, some were young, and some were middle-aged. There were about 29 male people present in total.

Each person, as John walked through one of the two different gates, was handed a white robe to put on and a pair of white slippers which were handed out at exactly the correct size of the person's feet they were being handed to. These males were all very confused although John seemed to have realized he must have died after his body had been pierced by the shot. It seemed obvious that this was the afterlife.

An elderly man introduced himself to John after he put on his robe and slippers. He claimed his name was "Matthew" and extended his hand to welcome John and shake his hand.

John asked, "What is this place?"

"You will be sitting down with these other men and all will be explained," Matthew responded.

John kept walking and following the other men down a long corridor. They soon came to a large conference room where everybody was asked to "take a seat."

Chapter Four

This was a very startling situation for John as he realized his life on Earth appeared to be over. It was over without him having lived the life he had once hoped for. As everybody present in the room sat down, a young man came on to the stage in front of them. He looked as if he was in his late 20's. He smiled as he began to speak to the small crowd in front of him.

"My name is William. I am one of God's assistants. God would like to see each one of you individually to introduce himself before you are released to an officer who will help you cope with the situation and refer you to your proper place here in the afterlife. I know. It all seems very confusing, but everything will make sense in due time."

God came on to the stage. A heavenly, seemingly middle-aged figure in a long white robe with greyish brown hair, God didn't say anything to the crowd as he took a place on the corner of the stage to stand. Each of the in-coming gentlemen present were instructed to walk on the stage to shake God's hand and continue walking afterwards straight through a door behind him on the stage.

When John's turn came to shake his hand, he was afraid the handshake might have been a "test," but the gesture turned out to be conducted perfectly. God looked into John's eyes for a second and John hoped that brief stare would ensure that all things would be as OK as possible given the circumstances. To be honest, John was afraid of hell and didn't know if he had done anything bad enough in his life to warrant a place there. That thought was assuming a place called hell even existed. From the looks of things, everything seemed peaceful.

When John walked through the door behind God, he saw a bright light and found himself on a cloud which was to take him to the next destination. When he arrived there, he was instructed by a woman to step off the cloud on to a beautiful light blue carpet in front of him.

"I'm Andrea. I'm your "officer" and I'll be here to answer any questions you may have regarding what I'm about to tell you."

Chapter Five

Andrea called John in to her office which was the only one on the floor he had stepped on to. John sat in a huge black seat with wheels on the bottom. He sat in front of the desk Andrea proceeded to sit behind.

"Do you have any questions for me?"

"Who are you?"

"My name is Andrea. I am your guide and will assign you the place you've been chosen to resign to for the next few weeks based upon a brief life "review.""

"Life review?"

"I have your file sitting in my desk. I read it quickly but know all the details very well. If there's something you'd like to say about your life on Earth that you think I should know, please tell me now."

"What are you looking at when you decide a person's situation?"

"Do you even know the situation you are in?"

"I do not."

"Well, you will."

"Can you tell me my situation?"

"I can tell you that you've died before your time and, unfortunately, your life review will therefore be an incomplete one."

"What does that mean for me?"

"You're a middle-aged man with no close family, few friends, and you have never truly sacrificed anything for anyone."

"I don't believe that to be true. In fact, I beg to differ. Also, can we go back a few pages? I have a question."

"What is it?"

"Where are my family and friends who are no longer among the living? Aren't they supposed to greet me at the entrance or something? Where are my parents?"

"You're not in Heaven. Although, even if you were, that idea seems to be wishful thinking on your part. Don't you think?"

"I wanted to see my parents."

"Your life isn't necessarily over on Earth."

"What do you mean?"

"I think we have to take some time to discuss the purpose of your life and what you wanted to get out of it versus what you actually did."

"I want to talk to your supervisor. It's not fair that you're telling me my life on Earth isn't over but here I am in what is obviously some form of the afterlife."

"My supervisor? There is only one person who I answer to and that's the big guy, himself."

"God?"

"You could call him God."

"What do you call him?"

"The voice of reason."

"I have a family. I have a sister."

"Meredith?"

"Good, let's start the conversation off with Meredith."

"What about Meredith? Why is she living on the other side of the country with a family of her own while you are stranded alone on the East coast?"

"It's a personal decision I made."

"Didn't Meredith offer you an apartment of your own in California to start your life over in several years back?"

"Yes, she did."

"She was going to pay for it."

"Correct."

"So, you were kind of selfish in that you turned down the offer."

"I didn't want to be a burden to her."

"If it would have been a burden to her, why would she have offered it?"

"I don't know. Let's go ahead and change the topic, please."

"Next on my list is the topic of vocation. Something you didn't really excel at in your life on Earth thus far."

"I always did excellent work in every job I ever held."

"Excellent to an extent. You never really excelled to the point of a promotion that would have made a substantial financial difference."

"Why are we talking about money?"

"Money is what they use in the country you were born in to measure success. We up here measure success in different ways but we always take into consideration the systems used places on Earth to measure success. If it works a lot on Earth, then there is some justification to believe it a reliable system of measuring one's merits. Wouldn't you agree?"

"I see."

"You were one who, even from an early age, didn't respect the system you were born into enough to make it work for yourself."

"I'm not sure I like where this is going."

Chapter Six

Back on Earth, Meredith had discovered the news of John's death. She and her husband, Richard, flew to New York City to identify the body. They left their two children with a babysitter they knew well. Meredith had not felt close to her brother since she was in her early 20's but wanted to give him a proper burial.

When they arrived in New York, they met a detective named Stanley Green who told them the story behind the shooting.

"It was a drug-addicted thief who shot John. He was fighting with some cops who were trying to apprehend him when a shot was fired. One shot that struck and killed John. I am so very sorry for your loss."

"Thank you," Meredith said as she saw John with his eyes closed in the body that she had hardly seen him in recently. She told her husband how much she wished she could have helped him more.

"I wanted to give him a better life than this."

"That was never your responsibility," Richard said.

"Not legally but morally, I felt that I could have been there for him more."

"Don't beat yourself up. It's not your fault some crazy guy shot him."

"I know but I could only imagine if he had said 'yes' to coming with us to California whether his life would have been a better one than the one he lived here."

"Don't do this to yourself. Let's just see about a proper funeral for him," Richard stated.

'I'm not sure many people would come."

"Even if it's just us, let's do the right thing."

"OK. I guess that would be best."

John was witnessing this occurrence as Andrea showed him from a TV monitor what was going on back on Earth with his sister. John was feeling very distressed. He had once planned on making a trip to see his sister for the holidays but cancelled it in order to get overtime at his job.

"Why are you showing me this, Andrea?"

"I want you to know the recent choices you made in your life. Do you think that you did the right thing by failing to communicate with your sister enough?"

"I did what I could do. I had to pay the bills. That was always the priority for me."

"Let's begin your life review, shall we?"

"Why not, Andrea? What else can you do to show me how awful my life was?"

"Let's begin with your childhood. Shall we? Do you think you were a good son?"

"I was an excellent son."

"Take it back to the early 1980's where you constantly begged your parents for Star Wars or He-Man toys. What did you do that time you wanted Orko, the toy from the Masters of the Universe collection?"

"I stole five dollars from my mother's purse."

"Good memory. I didn't even have to show you a film clip. Why did you do that?"

"I wanted the toy, and she wouldn't get it for me."

"You stole. You broke one of the 10 commandments."

"I didn't know the 10 commandments back then."

"On the contrary. I believe your father had taught them to you when you were five years old. Should I show you the tape?"

"Please, don't."

"Are you sorry for stealing your mother's hard-earned money to buy the toy before she could afford to buy it for you, herself?"

"Yes. I didn't realize that it would have been a burden on her."

"The next day, at work, your mother went to use the five dollars to buy Roy Rogers by her job and the money wasn't there."

"Did she eat that day?"

"She did. She used change to pay for her meal. Change that, luckily, you didn't steal from her."

"In this life review, is there any possibility that I may forward time to when I was 15?"

"Why would you want to fast forward the review? I want to analyze the things you did and didn't do during your entire life."

"I have a question for God. I want to ask him, "Why, when I wanted this girl from high school to like me more than anything else in the whole entire world, he decided to let her say 'no' when I asked her if she liked me back?"

"Free will of the human being you liked has nothing to do with God."

"I wanted her to like me more than anything else in the whole entire world and I prayed to God for months before I wrote her a note asking her if she liked me."

"People pray to God every day. He can't answer everyone's prayers the way these people want them to be answered."

"But he's God, isn't he? He should be able to."

"I think you have a misperception of who, exactly, God is. He is here to manage things in Heaven and on Earth, and to make sure people do the right thing. He listens and he gives things to people, but he can't give things to everyone just because these people want the things that they want. He honors the important wishes of people who really need him, most of the time. Whenever possible, he does the best he can."

"His best wasn't good enough for me. Because when he let this girl whose name was Molly, as you probably know, reject me, he took both of my parents away from me just a short time later when they died."

"I know you have suffered. When I was given your file, I didn't want your case. I knew you had been dealt an unfair hand at life. I will also have to examine the things that you did have control of yourself. These are times in your life that you probably didn't make the right decisions, especially when confronted with problems. Yours is a tough case. I'd argue Heaven for you, initially. but the more I look at your file, the more I question the things that you had done in your life on Earth."

Chapter Seven

John and Andrea were looking at a screen where John, as a 14-year old teenager, discovered the first girl he had liked, Molly. John was timidly avoiding her upon their first interaction and Andrea asked him why it was, if he liked her so much, that he decided to avoid speaking to her when she asked him for a pencil sharpener.

"I was shy."

"Shy doesn't get people what they want in life. You were smart enough, even at that age, to know this."

"I want another chance."

"I hear that 10 times a day on a slow day. There is a plan for you here in the afterlife."

"I don't want to know the plan. I want you to help me out here. Why can't I get another shot at life on Earth?"

"If you used this kind of aggressiveness with Molly, you would have been married with children by now, for sure. Don't you think?"

"I know what you're saying."

"If we sent you back, which is only a tiny possibility, you would forget everything. You would start from scratch."

"I know. That's all I want. Another chance."

"I'll talk to the Big Guy. That's all I can really do here. You're being uncooperative as I was told you may be. I see this behavior a few times almost every single day. Sometimes, the Big Guy lets certain people have a 'do-over.' I'll see what I can do. Please wait outside the office. There's a chair right in front of my door."

John waited as he sat in the seat outside Andrea's office. Andrea stepped onto a cloud that went upwards towards the sky. John was nervous and was thinking that he may not get another chance at life. Andrea had made some valid points, in his opinion, regarding what he had done wrong in his life on Earth.

About ten minutes later, Andrea came down off the cloud and called John back into her office. John followed her in with great skepticism.

"You won't remember this conversation after about ten minutes from now but you're going back to Earth. You will be born on Earth once again and you will have 40-years to find a wife, a family, and a good job to support them. If that's what you want to happen, we'll make it happen. If you don't, we'll move forward with our original plan."

"No. I like the new plan. How do you actually plan to send me back to Earth?"

"We have our ways. Don't ask questions you know we will not give you the answers to."

"But, if I'm going to forget anyway, why not just tell me?

"If you're going to forget anyway, why do you care? You make no sense."

A man in a white uniform entered the room. Andrea told him to administer the shot which would put John's body to rest.

John was scared as the man gave him an injection. Andrea told John as the shot was being administrated that everything was going to be OK. He believed her as he fell into a deep sleep and there was a blank, black image in John's mind. Life seemed to stop. Everything came to a silent halt.

Chapter Eight

A baby boy was being born in a Brooklyn hospital to one Megan Taylor. She was 35-years old and had just married the father who was the same age. She had met him through an online dating site. Josh was the dad's name. The baby was crying hysterically as it came out of her and into the world. When Megan was finally able to hold the baby, she held him close to her. Megan started to cry, herself, and wished Josh could have been there as well. He was working at his legal assistant job in New York City.

Being happier than she ever was before, Megan, a full-time nursing student, eventually left the hospital by Josh's side a few days later. As they were the proud new parents of the baby, they wanted nothing more than to celebrate its arrival and select, for him, a strong name. They chose the name Peter for the little guy.

One day a few months later, Megan and Josh were taking Peter in a carriage to the supermarket. Peter, almost three months old, stared out of the carriage and the world surrounding him seemed so very peculiar. Bright lights from the sky shined into the carriage and he could see his parents peeking in on him from time to time. As they wheeled him through Brooklyn's Williamsburg area, the parents were discussing amongst themselves what was going on.

"We can't afford the rental on our apartment anymore if I quit my job and school to watch Peter," Megan stated.

"I'm looking for something better. There are a lot of firms in the city. Just bear with me a little while longer, darling," Josh replied.

"I don't know how long we could hold out for. The prices of everything for the baby is adding up. I just maxed out the credit card buying diapers and wipes for Peter."

"I'll request credit line increases then. We pay our bills. We always have."

"I know. I was just a little worried."

"Don't be. Stay in school and work less hours. That's the only thing you can do for now."

"What about a nanny?"

"I'll look into it."

"Please do. I'm not sure I like the babysitter we're using. She's always talking on the phone to her boyfriend when I listen in the door before I announce that I'm home. Sometimes, even when the baby is crying, she ignores him to talk to her boyfriend."

"Why didn't you tell me that. I thought she had experience."

"She probably did. I never called her references, though. I went on the ones that were on the website we got her from."

"Don't worry today. I'll see what I can do," Josh said.

Josh was carrying the baby carriage up the stairs to their 3rd floor apartment in Brooklyn. Megan was carrying the baby in her arms and walking up the stairs behind him. A tall, male 29-year-old renter of an apartment from the 4th floor was bringing his huge bicycle down the stairs and as he approached the third floor, he lost the grip of the bike and it went tumbling down the stairs on its own. Josh was on the second floor when he heard the guy who owned the bike yell, "Watch out!"

Josh didn't know what was going on and, as the bike came spinning down the stairs, he told Megan to step to the side of the staircase with the baby as Josh tried to get a grip on the carriage and move it to the side as well. However, the bike ran into the carriage and Josh let go grabbing on to the banister instead to support himself as the bicycle hit the carriage and both the bike and the carriage went tumbling down the stairs together.

Josh grabbed Megan the first chance he got to see if she was OK and it seemed that neither she nor Peter had been hurt. The owner of the bike, whose name was Jeff, apologized and went to get his bike. Josh went down a flight to see about his carriage and it was apparently not affected much. Jeff said he was "sorry" again and went off with his bicycle as Josh continued to carry the stroller up the stairs again.

"That was scary," Megan told him as Peter started crying.

"We'll get out of here once the lease is up," Josh replied.

"Just thank God we're both OK," he continued.

Chapter Nine

Megan was happy that, in less than a year's time, Josh managed to move them out to a house on Long Island. Megan had finished school but was not working anymore. She was going to watch Peter full-time until he was of the age to go to school. They couldn't afford a nanny or daycare, but Josh had excellent credit that helped them secure the mortgage for the house. Josh was now working extra hours at a new firm in Manhattan. His salary was better. They both settled into the parent lifestyle in a different environment that the one they were previously living in. They were happy, however, as Peter grew up quite content and happy.

When he entered third grade, Peter was doing extremely well with reading, and math and won a Student of the Month award. Peter felt familiar with his school activities and it was almost as if he had been exposed to the material before the time he was actually presented with it. He was absorbing material at a rapid pace as Peter's female teacher, Ms. Riley, pointed out to Megan during a parent teacher conference.

By the time, Peter entered fifth grade, he had developed a crush on his classmate, Sarah. She wore glasses and had long, braided hair. Her smile simply made Peter happy and he felt a connection to her he couldn't explain as he discussed his feelings with his mother who was driving him to school that morning.

"Mom, why do I feel these weird things inside for this girl in my class?"

"What's the girl's name?"

"Sarah."

"Well, there comes a time in every boy's life where he starts to become a man and liking a girl is the first step,"

"What do you mean, exactly, mommy?"

"I'll let your dad explain when you come home later, OK, Peter?"

"OK, Mom," Peter said as he stepped out of the car and went over to his two male friends who he had not yet told about his secret crush on Sarah.

Later on in the evening, Megan, Josh and Peter were seated at the dinner table. Peter brought up the subject of boys and girls. Josh, who had a long day at work, was not ready for that particular discussion at the present time.

"Peter, worry about your schoolwork and not about girls. That's the problem with kids today, if you ask me," Josh said.

"Don't be so hard on him," Megan replied.

"I just don't get why I feel the way I do when I'm around Sarah," Peter responded.

"In two more years, I'll have a discussion with you on that topic. For now, focus on getting good marks. That's all I ask."

"OK, Dad."

Megan looked at Peter and smiled before looking at Josh who seemed stressed out that evening. Josh, who had a look of distress on his face, looked away and continued to eat his dinner. After dinner, Josh excused himself from the table and went to his bedroom to sleep.

While Peter seemed curious about everything that was going on in regard to his liking of girls, he had no choice but to keep the thoughts he had secret in his head as the next few months progressed. He felt odd talking about such things with his young male friends who he more importantly wanted to play baseball with. Peter wanted to get into little league and saw any practice he could get as pivotal to making that dream come true.

In religion classes Peter took on Sundays before family mass, he had questions that he wanted to ask the teacher. He had questions about a lot of different things on his mind. He recently made his first communion and didn't fully understand why that was important.

Peter's Catholic religion teacher, Ms. Evans, didn't want to answer the question Peter approached her with after class one Sunday. That question was, again, in regard to why boys like girls and why girls like boys.

Chapter 10

Peter learned through religion class in the next year that the reason boys and girls liked each other was they needed each other to fall in love and get married in order to have a family. Peter started to like the idea of "soul mates" which was introduced to him on a Disney Plus television show he had recently watched.

Peter wanted to ask Sarah out so much that it hurt him inside whenever he thought of her. He didn't know where he would take her and only had a few dollars saved in his piggy bank but he wanted to have lunch with Sarah one day outside of the school grounds.

It was difficult for Peter to muster up the courage to ask her out and, one day, Sarah stopped coming to school. It was announced to the class that she had moved to another state when a curious student asked the teacher one day.

In Peter's dreams, he could occasionally see Sarah's smile. One night while he was in dreamland, a man approached him in a robe. This man had long brown hair and a beard and asked Peter to sit down beside him.

"You're having a hard time, Peter."

"Who are you?"

"I am God."

"God, why are you here?"

"To tell you there's a reason you feel things so deeply and I want you to act on your feelings, not hold them in."

"Why, God? Why should I act on things I feel when my father told me the other day that doing that causes problems?

"Your father has a hard life, but he has made his dreams come true by marrying your mother and having you."

"I want to be with my mom and dad, but I want to have a girlfriend of my own one day."

"Please, Peter, next time you are given the chance to feel something strong, act on that feeling, OK?"

"Yes, God," Peter replied as he felt someone shaking him.

When Peter opened his eyes, he saw it was his father, Josh. His dad was waking him up so he could get to school on time that morning.

Megan drove Peter to school and in the car, Peter asked about God and told his mother about his dream.

"Does God ever come to you in your dreams, Mom?"

"No, why, has he come to you in your dreams?"

"Yes. He told me in my dream to act on the way I feel next time. I think he meant with a girl because I was thinking about Sarah last night before I fell asleep."

"Dreams are fun while they're happening, and they make us feel happy while we sleep, but they are just fake. Focus on your math test today. That's what's real right now."

"I see, Mom. It was just a dream then. It wasn't real."

"That's right, Peter," Megan said as her son prepared to get out of the car to go to school.

Peter thought about his dream all day long. Although he rarely remembered his dreams, this time, he couldn't forget since it pertained to Sarah who he had such deep feelings for despite hardly knowing her whole personality. Peter had an appreciation for her looks but seemed to think it was more of a connection that it may actually have been. He wasn't sure how strong the connection was for Sarah, but he was feeling things that seemed beyond his control.

Over the next few nights, Peter tried to dream of God again but had no such luck. He dreamt of things based on the video games he played, or the television shows he watched. God was not coming back to see him in dreamland although Peter wanted nothing more than to discuss with God how he was feeling emotionally. His attachment to Sarah seemed quite unusual to him.

Chapter 11

As the years passed and Peter became a teenager, he had many interactions with girls but never seemed to feel the yearning to get to know any of them. It was hard for him to feel the way he had felt about Sarah with another girl. It didn't make much sense, so Peter focused on his studies and got good grades. All through high school, there were no other girls he felt a connection to and although there were opportunities for girlfriends, he didn't seize any of them. Instead, he elected to hold on to the thought that, perhaps, Sarah was his soul mate and that he would see her again.

Megan and Josh were currently fighting about where to send Peter to college. Although Peter wanted to go to a private school in Manhattan, his parents had a state college on Long Island in mind.

"I don't want you to have to work long shifts to pay tuition," Josh explained to Megan.

"That demotion you got last month really hurt us," Megan replied.

"I can still carry the mortgage and Peter could get scholarships for the cheaper schools. I know it."

"Isn't it about what Peter wants?"

"He's 17. He doesn't' know what he wants, just like we didn't know what we wanted at that age either. We ended up in the wrong schools and I don't want the same for Peter," Josh stated.

"Peter understands. I told him to go to Stony Brook. We'll see what he does," Megan said.

Peter was wrestling with his feelings and didn't really want to go to college. He wanted to get a job and find a girl like Sarah, if not Sarah herself. Although his parents were pretty demanding that he go to some kind of college, Peter was uncertain what he wanted to do professionally. He had a yearning to do things his parents had told him were unrealistic. Peter's grades were all 90's but he didn't excel at any particular thing. He was good in school but only did what was expected of him because it was what was presented to him. He didn't like any of his classes with any kind of special passion.

It came as no surprise to Peter that he went to Stony Brook as per his parents' wishes. He had no choice being that he didn't have a major in mind. Living on campus and taking courses which didn't interest him, his grades dwindled from the ones he received in high school. He was losing interest in the subjects that were being taught to him.

One summer, he got a job as a camp counselor and found he enjoyed working with kids. He wanted to start taking education courses in college but with two more years of school facing him, he decided instead to leave school due to low overall marks. He told his mom this information before junior year was going to start.

"I'm tired of school, Mom. I'm going to get a job."

"What are you going to do? Daddy was going to pay the tuition tomorrow."

"Well, I was going to see who's hiring. Do you mind if I borrow the car and drive around?"

"C'mon, Peter. Your father and I thought you had so much potential to finish school."

"What gave you that idea? My "C+" average?"

"We thought you were in a slump and that you'd grow out of it once you found a major you liked."

"I don't think I got anything higher than a "B" in any topic so that idea of 'majoring' in something isn't going to work."

"I see. I guess when you tell your father, you can explain it to him."

"I thought maybe you could explain it to him."

"It's your decision and I can't get inside your head to explain it the way you could."

"It's simple. I'm ready to start life. I haven't made any real friends, I have no girlfriend, I need to carve a path for myself."

"You'll talk to him. I better call him before he writes that tuition check."

Chapter 12

Josh came home from work that evening and confronted Peter. Josh was quite upset with Peter's decision.

"You're going to finish school. I just worked twenty hours of overtime this week to pay the tuition, OK?"

"C'mon, Dad. You're wasting your money. I don't want school anymore. I can't meet anyone I relate to and no girl I think is attractive is available. It's like torture to me."

"School is your life. It can secure you a future, so you don't have to struggle like I do."

"I'll struggle to find the life I actually want, and I don't care how hard I have to fight to get what I want."

"You're disappointing your mom and I so much. I can live with your decision if it's what you really want. We could really use the tuition money for our bills."

"See. I'm actually helping you guys out."

"Don't make a decision based on money. You know we'd always pay for whatever it is that you want."

"I know that."

When Josh went to go talk to Megan about his acceptance of Peter's decision, Peter went to his room and closed the door. Peter wanted to dream again even though he didn't remember the dreams he would have at night. He knew he felt something surreal in his dreams. He couldn't explain anything to his parents other than the fact that sleeping at night gave him peace. When he woke up, he would feel disappointed that he couldn't remember the dreams that would excite him while he slept.

Peter had the thought one day he would find Sarah again and see if she had feelings for him similar to the ones he seemed to have for her. Peter drove around Long Island one afternoon and although there were Help Wanted signs on several windows, he decided to try to get a better paying job in Manhattan. Even though he would have to take the Long Island Railroad to work, he wanted to earn more than minimum wage.

Peter's college coursework and camp counselor experience helped him get an administrative job at an art school in lower Manhattan. He was hired after his interview based on his appealing personality. The school's headmaster, Mrs. Higgins, found him to be very personable and believed he would get along well with the staff and students at the school. Peter's parents were proud as their son would begin his life as a commuter working in the big city.

On his lunch break one Wednesday afternoon, Peter was sitting in a Starbucks in the city with his laptop opened. Peter was on the internet using the store's Wi-Fi as he looked on a dating site to see if anybody appealed to him. He saw a woman he thought was pretty on the website but when he clicked to answer her ad, the website was asking for a credit card account number to pay the $29 membership fee. He logged off the website and went on YouTube to listen to music videos.

During Peter's dream the following night while he was sleeping, he saw a violent scenario occurring at a train station and then felt uneasy. Police were running after a man with a gun in the dream. Peter got up and got a drink of water before returning to sleep. He had rarely had nightmares before that night, but this vision seemed different to him from other bad dreams he had experienced in the past.

Peter remembered the night God came to him in his dream and told him to act on how he felt. He was acting on his feelings the way he believed was right by getting the new job and working in the city. He wished he could act on romantic feelings he had towards somebody special but there was no such person in his life at the current moment.

Eventually, after a couple of months, Peter decided to move to Queens to be closer to his job. His parents were saddened on what was seemingly the last day he would spend living in their home.

"You can visit any time you want," Megan told him.

Josh asked, "Why would he want to visit?"

"Of course, I'll visit, Dad," Peter said.

"They're laying people off at my job," Josh stated.

"Well, if you need to move in with me, I'll make space for you guys on the couch."

"That's not what I meant. It's just that everything must happen for a reason in life. I'm not sure if we had to pay that tuition that things would have worked out as smoothly as we would have wanted them to," Josh said.

"Are you guys thinking about selling the house?"

"Absolutely not," Megan said.

"I'll miss you guys," Peter stated.

Megan gave Peter a hug. Josh was going to drive some of Peter's stuff to the city and as they left Megan, they could notice she was understandably upset.

"I'll call you, Mom."

"Thanks, baby. Good luck with everything. I hope you find whatever it is you're looking for."

Josh and Peter went outside and got in the car which was filled with Peter's belongings. Peter had purchased some new furniture for his apartment already and it had already been set up. He was just bringing some of his personal items to Queens in order to start his new life.

That night, Peter felt lonely. He missed his parents and knew that one day, he would want to have children of his own. Peter logged into his computer and went on to a dating website. He couldn't wait to meet someone in "real life" anymore. He had to meet someone nice. He was going to try to do things virtually for the time being and see if he could find someone interesting to get to know.

At work the next morning, Mrs. Higgins assigned Peter some heavy projects, one of which included organizing the essays for the scholarship the school was going to be giving out. One scholarship recipient was going to be selected based on the essays prospective students were submitting to the school. Mrs. Higgins wanted him to summarize each essay in one sentence. He was to write that summary on a sticky note and attach it to each file. It seemed mundane but Peter got used to the task rather quickly. This school for which he worked offered some of the best in undergraduate art programs which ultimately led to a BFA degree. However, some of the essays didn't really capture what the student ultimately wanted to do there. Peter started becoming very critical of some of the essays and wrote his own personal notes on a separate piece of paper.

Peter came across a prospective undergraduate student named Sylvia McAvoy. Her essay was the strongest one he read since it re-enforced Sylvia's personal religious beliefs. However, the school did not have a religious affiliation which made his attachment to the themes of the paper very personal. One section of her essay read as follows:

In believing in God, I've found the strength to pursue my creative talents and put them to good use. Through the programs your institution offers, I believe I could find who I truly am as a person. I have a good idea of who I am but it's which side of my creative talents that I want to show the public which intrigues me most of all. I truly believe I could flourish there if given the opportunity.

Peter looked Sylvia's profile up on Facebook and saw her photo was that of a beautiful young woman who had just graduated high school. She had long curly brown hair and glasses and seemed so full of joy in her online photos. He also noticed that she had a baby daughter. Peter wanted to know more but closed out the Facebook page as Mrs. Higgins walked in. He summarized Sylvia's essay in a sentence and moved on to the next essay contest participant's paper.

Chapter 13

When he was home, he looked at dating website profiles but, for some odd reason, couldn't get his mind off of Sylvia. Peter believed in God with the same passions he believed Sylvia did, and he wondered about the story behind Sylvia's daughter's birth. He also was curious as to whether or not Sylvia was still with the father of the baby. It felt unusual to him to possess a bond with anyone but, in this particular case, it wasn't a good idea to mix business with pleasure. That is if you could call his interest in her pleasure.

Peter had been introduced to Sylvia through his job and it was initially his intention to keep all interest in her purely professional. When he clicked to send her a private message on Facebook, he realized his profile stated where he worked so he held back on sending the message.

When he went to sleep that night, he had visions of the images of he saw of Sylvia online and felt passionately towards her based on the words she had written in her essay. It was an unusual feeling for Peter, but he accepted what he felt towards this girl he had never met and enjoyed dreaming of a real-life connection with her. When he woke up the next morning, he was saddened to see the dream end.

As time progressed, and two weeks passed, Mrs. Higgins had read all the essays for the scholarship contest and asked Peter which one he had liked the most. Peter's decision wouldn't really matter but she was curious as to what he thought. Peter told her he enjoyed Sylvia's the best although he admitted his response to her essay may have been based on her religious values which were similar to his own.

"It's so funny that you should say that Peter," Mrs. Higgins said.

"Why is it funny?"

"I felt she had a great vocabulary and ideas flowed tremendously well in her essay. She was second on my list."

"I guess great minds think alike."

"Very funny, Peter. I'll have the board review all the essays and we're going to call in the top three candidates for in-person interviews."

"That sounds great."

"I'll let you know by the end of the week and you are to set up the interviews, OK?"

"OK."

About a week later, Sylvia was picked by Mrs. Higgins and the school's board to be one of the top three candidates for the scholarship prize the school offered. Peter was designated to reach out to Sylvia to inform her about an upcoming in-person interview which would help determine if she would ultimately win the full 4-year scholarship to the school.

Peter called Sylvia and the two male candidates who were also in competition for the scholarship. He let them all know they were finalists and set up an individual interview time slot for each of the three candidates which would occur on the following Tuesday.

Sylvia had answered the phone with her soft voice, sounding absolutely sublime to Peter. She had an elegance and sophistication he discovered in her voice that was a stark contrast to the two gentlemen he called who seemed more ordinary to him for some reason. Sylvia was the one who he was hoping would win the scholarship. In her essay, Sylvia expressed an interest in the film program the school offered, and she cited that she liked taking photographs and loved the art of acting. It seemed like she was in the lead for the scholarship from what he overheard in Mrs. Higgins' office as well.

On the day that the interviews were set to take place, Peter made sure to dress extremely well and even wore a tie just in case he would cross paths with Sylvia. He knew he would see her in the lobby when she came in and that she'd probably have contact with him as his office was right across from the waiting area.

The first candidate, George, showed up for his interview on time. George had a stocky build and long blonde hair. He was tall and looked much younger than Peter had imagined him to be from reading his essay. Peter knew George was graduating high school that year but from the look of him, he seemed like he was just starting high school.

Sylvia showed up just as George entered the office to speak to Mrs. Higgins. When he saw her walking towards the office, Peter came over to her and introduced himself.

"Hi, you must be Ms. McAvoy. I'm Peter. I assist Mrs. Higgins. Congratulations on making the final three. Mrs. Higgins will be with you shortly. Just have a seat right over there."

"No problem. Pleased to meet you," she said as she sat down.

Peter walked away hoping he made a good impression. Sylvia had been smiling during their introduction and he kept the image of her smile in his head as he returned to his desk. When George left Mrs. Higgins' office, Peter thought she seemed pleased with the interview she had just conducted. Peter knew, though, that Sylvia possessed a radiance like very few other girls he had encountered in his life had. Peter hoped Mrs. Higgins would see the same qualities in Sylvia that he did as Mrs. Higgins invited Sylvia into her office and closed the door.

Chapter 14

When all three interviews were completed, Peter was curious to get an answer from Mrs. Higgins as to who she would select for the scholarship. Mrs. Higgins, however, kept the door to her office shut and didn't discuss the matter with anyone for days. As she would assign Peter tasks, he would anxiously await her response regarding who she had selected but an answer didn't come for days. He was afraid of asking her directly because he didn't want to get a response which he would be disappointed with.

Peter had looked Sylvia up on Facebook a few times and saw her daughter was almost a year old but there was no marital status presented on the page nor was there any information regarding whether she was single or not. Even if she wasn't available to him, he wanted to get to know her for some reason. He wanted to have some kind of friendship with her even if it didn't lead to anything further.

At work, Mrs. Higgins announced that she was calling two of the three candidates for the scholarship back. She wanted to interview one of the gentlemen she had met again because she felt she had rushed his interview, and she needed to talk to Sylvia one more time before she would be able to make a final decision. This time, she called the two candidates herself to schedule the interviews. They would be held one day apart from each other.

Peter wondered why Mrs. Higgins called the candidates herself and why he, himself, had to call George to tell him he wasn't selected for the scholarship. It didn't seem fair to Peter that he had to give the bad news out but then Peter realized he, himself, didn't even have a college degree so it was only fair that it was he who was selected to deliver the bad news to George.

When Peter dialed the first six digits of George's number, he stopped dialing and hung up the phone. He went to go knock on Mrs. Higgins' door to see why the school couldn't just send George a letter stating he was rejected for the scholarship.

Peter knocked on Mrs. Higgins' door.

"Come in, Peter."

"Mrs. Higgins, why don't we just send George a letter telling him he didn't get the scholarship? Wouldn't that be so much easier?"

"Easier, yes. But we pay you to do work around here and why should we waste a stamp when you can simply call George and let him know?"

"Don't you think an official notification in writing would be preferable for George?"

"Why don't you call him and ask him?"

"Why would I do that?"

"It's your choice, Peter. Don't mention writing a letter to him on the phone, just give him the news."

"OK. I'll call him."

"You should have called him five minutes ago. We're wasting time here," Mrs. Higgins replied.

Peter went back into his office and called George and when he answered, George seemed enthusiastic as he said "hello." It was almost as if George had been waiting for the phone call to come.

"Hi. It's Peter from the offices here at the college. Mrs. Higgins wanted me to thank you for coming in and let you know that they went with another candidate for the scholarship."

"I see. Thanks anyway," George said.

"Good luck, and we appreciate all your efforts," Peter replied before abruptly hanging up the phone.

He didn't hear if George said anything back. Peter was too uncomfortable making the call. He got the message across to George and that was good enough for Peter.

When Sylvia came back for her second interview, she looked even more radiant to Peter than she did the first time. She had on a pair of diamond earrings and a lovely dark sweater. Sylvia also had stockings on with black shoes. Peter admired her beauty but simply sat in his office this time. He didn't go out to greet Sylvia as Mrs. Higgins noticed her presence by the office almost immediately.

Sylvia wasn't in the office more than five minutes before she was dismissed by Mrs. Higgins. Peter had an uneasy feeling and didn't want to pursue the answer to the question he had regarding what was said by Sylvia in the interview.

When the next day arrived, Li, a Chinese student who was the other scholarship candidate, came to Mrs. Higgins' office. Li had a lengthy thirty-minute interview with her. After Li came out, Peter knew who was going to be selected for the scholarship. Li shook Mrs. Higgins' hand ever so tightly and it looked from, within Peter's office, that the deal had been officially sealed.

Chapter 15

Peter believed his dreams had been shattered. Although Li turned out to be an excellent student when he started his first year as a film major, Peter believed not giving the scholarship to Sylvia was a mistake. Peter had hoped Sylvia would have still attended the school but according to the school's records, she was not currently enrolled there as a student.

Peter sporadically checked Sylvia's Facebook page for updates. It seemed, with the exception of new baby pictures, that Sylvia's profile didn't offer its visitors any more information on her personal life. It would seem odd for Peter to request her as a friend on the website now being that he had already missed the chance to do so when Sylvia had the potential to be a student at the school in which he worked.

However, one day at work, it was really quiet, and Peter found himself in Mrs. Higgins' office putting some school files on her desk. He recently noticed Li had even gotten an internship on the same floor as him near the admissions office. Peter decided to ask Mrs. Higgins about Sylvia and why she chose Li over her.

"I remember Li was competing against that girl, Sylvia. How did you decide between Li and Sylvia, anyway for the scholarship?"

"It was always Li. Sylvia told me when she first met me that her daughter came first. I always understood it, but nobody gets a BFA with a 3.5 grade point average in film supporting a daughter."

"What do you mean?"

"She couldn't handle it. She told me so herself. Don't you have something to fax somewhere?"

"No. I don't. Well, take those files over there, alphabetize them and fax me all the cover sheets. I need everything within the hour."

"No problem, Mrs. Higgins," Peter said.

About six months later, Peter's position had been reduced to part-time and Li took over doing much of Peter's work for no pay, just school credit. Two months after that, Peter's position was permanently eliminated from the school's budget. Mrs. Higgins gave Peter an envelope that had a letter inside about the lay-off. She didn't even say anything to him other than "Good luck" when he left.

Peter called his mom to tell her the news. Megan had gone back to work as a nurse and was devastated that Peter had lost his job,

"Don't worry, Peter. You'll get unemployment. We'll work everything out. Do you want to keep the apartment or break the lease? Maybe daddy can help."

"I want to stay here in Queens. I'll find something. I can't believe my luck. Everything seemed to be going so well and then, boom."

"Do you have any girlfriends?"

"C'mon, Mom. Don't ask me that."

"What does that supposed to mean?"

"No, Mom. No girlfriend."

"Should I have Dad call you?"

"No. There's no need for that. Let me send out some resumes and see what happens."

"OK, dear. Please call us if you need anything."

"Will do," Peter said.

Peter felt lost. Every time he attached any sort of feelings to anything substantial, he seemed to lose what he felt he liked the most about life. He liked Sarah, Sylvia, and his job and all three things had vanished almost as quickly as they had come into his life.

Finding another job proved to be problematic. Although he spent time praying in church on Sundays each weekend, nothing he asked God for seemed to be coming his way anytime soon. He decided to not pay the next month's rent that was due because it would have left his bank account empty.

Chapter 16

While Peter was behind a month's rent and applying for new jobs, he felt compelled to do something productive with his life. Doing something productive, however, didn't necessarily mean he only wanted to do something that earned an income. Although he needed money, Peter wanted to feel some sort of importance regarding his life. He wanted to feel like his life mattered to someone other than himself and his parents. He stopped by the local church in his Queens neighborhood. He asked the secretary near the rectory if there was anything that he could do to help the church.

"How long have you been in the parish?" Joyce, the 35-year-old secretary asked him.

"I've come to masses. Today's my first inquiry into actually joining the parish, I guess."

"Are you interested in becoming a member?"

"Yes, but there's more to it than that."

"What do you mean?"

"I want to get involved. How can I get involved?"

"Do you come to mass every Sunday?"

"Yes, I do."

"You might want to look into joining some groups we have here."

"What kind of groups?"

"If you don't mind me asking, are you 18?"

"I'm older than 18 by quite a few years."

"Great. We have a young adult group that meets on Wednesdays. You may be perfect for it."

"What does the group do?"

"They meet and talk about problems, God, things like that. Usually, there's about 10 people in their late teens or early 20's that come to those meetings."

"That would be interesting."

"Fill out this form and we'll get you registered with the parish. Then, you can come to the groups. What parish are you from?"

"I went to church on Long Island before I started coming here."

"Oh, you're from the Island?"

"Yes."

"Do you have a pen?"

"I do," Peter said as he pulled a pen out of his pocket and began filling out the form to become a parish member.

Peter was excited about the prospect of meeting new people. When he showed up for the first group on the following Wednesday night at 7 PM, he saw three young ladies waiting outside the door where the meeting was going to be held.

"I'm Peter," he said as he introduced himself to the girls, one of whom responded that her name was Jennifer.

Jennifer was 20 years old, had long brown hair and braces, and went to a city college in Manhattan. Her friends were Anne, 18-years-old, and Debbie, who was 22.

Peter felt he was most interested in Jennifer but thought her friends looked nice as well. He couldn't wait to get to know them better as the other group members started to arrive. There was a total of five guys in the group. There were six girls.

One of the young ladies in the group was named Melanie, 24, and she wore jeans with tears in them. She was a little overweight. She looked very friendly and approachable to Peter.

A 41-year-old Sunday school teacher named Mrs. Downey ran the group and she was excited to welcome Peter to the group as he was the only first-timer there tonight. She asked Peter to introduce himself.

"I'm Peter. I have strong faith in God and believe I have a purpose which is why I decided to come tonight. I was hoping maybe I could make a difference by doing something great here with the group."

"What do you do?"

"I worked for an art school in the city. I recently lost my job. I'm looking for something new. I'm hoping this group may be an inspiration for me to find out what I want to do with the rest of my life."

"I've seen you at mass, Peter," Debbie replied.

"I think I've seen you too," Peter said.

Mrs. Downey had the group introduce themselves to Peter. Everyone was really nice. Peter learned Anne had just graduated high school and was dating a guy named Paul who worked for National Grid and was six years older than her. They wanted to get married and start a family.

Mrs. Downey asked, "Do you want to have a family one day?"

"One day," Peter said.

"I just need to find a new job and settle in first," he continued.

"You'll find something. If anyone hears of any job opportunities for Peter, please let him know next week," Mrs. Downey stated.

"Sounds great," Peter said.

They continued the group by saying a prayer. It was the "Our Father." Peter started to remember the times God seemed to have visited him in his dreams. He felt compelled to tell the group about his experiences.

"Has anybody ever dreamt of God? Sometimes I feel he comes to me while I sleep at night."

Anne asked, "What do you mean?"

"I just feel that He contacts me. I don't know what we talk about. I wake up and then I forget everything."

"Just like all dreams. They're so hard to remember," Debbie said.

"I feel like He's trying to tell me something."

"Peter, what is it that you think He's trying to tell you?" Jennifer asked.

"How to live a better life, maybe. I can't be sure."

"I wouldn't worry too much," Mrs. Downey responded.

"Why not?"

"I think if you live life like God has taught us to then you'll eventually find your way. So nice to meet you, Peter," Mrs. Downey said.

For the rest of the time of the group session, the other people in the room spoke while Peter listened attentively. The group, Peter learned, welcomed people up to age 29. He said "goodbye" to the group as it ended, and everyone got up to leave. As he walked out, Peter felt that he finally found something he was happy to be a part of in his life.

Chapter 17

Peter couldn't wait for next week's group to try to obtain employment. He was scrambling to find some kind of job. He had administrative experience behind him, but the ads he answered on the job search engines weren't leading to any incoming phone calls. Peter stopped by a weekday morning mass to pray for God's help finding new employment. During the mass, he felt safe and that an answer to his prayer would come soon. There were mostly senior citizens present at the church that day which made Peter feel he was alone in terms of being surrounded by people his own age. Although, he was sad, he remained hopeful as he left the church.

When he slept, he had visions of being attacked on a subway platform. He felt older in his dream than he actually was, and almost felt he really died as a result of the attack he was dreaming about. Peter sometimes tried to wake himself up during bad dreams but this time, he didn't try. He wanted to see where the vision was heading. About a minute before his alarm went off, Peter saw clouds and felt he was running in his dream jumping from various clouds to new clouds quite quickly. When the alarm finally went off, Peter was shaking. He had never felt he was actually part of a dream as he did in those moments he experienced while sleeping.

Although he wanted to have job leads at his next young adult group meeting to impress everyone, he didn't have any as the next group gathering arrived. Peter, who was wearing a New York Mets hat that night, was the first to arrive this time as he waited outside the door of the room the meeting was to be held in. Jennifer was next to arrive and although he liked her personality and looks judging from the last group, he wasn't going to admit anything like that to her that night. Peter tried to make interesting small talk, but Jennifer was busy texting her friends and only gave one-word answers to the questions he asked her. When he asked her how she was doing she simply said, "Fine."

When everybody was present at the group and the atmosphere in the room seemed similar to the way it seemed last week, Peter was determined to bring up an interesting topic of conversation. He felt he was always a good conversation starter, but he didn't know what quite to say as Debbie started talking about a term paper on psychology she was struggling with in college.

Although things seemed to go well in the group that night, Peter didn't get to speak as much as he had hoped. He was afraid of revealing his internal struggles to the group and kept his dialogue focused on simple things like the changes in weather that were coming up later in the week. Although he was with people in his age range, he started to notice a certain level of immaturity in some of the group members. Peter realized he had dropped out of school and most of the people in the group were still students. Although he wished he never left college, he realized that if he never left, he never would have found that group.

As Peter was leaving, he noticed he forgot the baseball cap he had worn that night. He had taken it off when the group started. He walked back towards the room, and heard Mrs. Downey talking to Jennifer. Instead of walking any further, he stopped and listened.

"Well, I wanted to thank you again for the advice," Jennifer said.

"Anytime," Mrs. Downey replied as she pointed to the baseball cap that was on the chair next to her.

"That's that guy, Peter's hat. I don't know about that guy. Something about him makes me feel uneasy. He doesn't go to school or work. That's weird."

"You know these new people come and go in group. He'll probably get a new job soon. I doubt he'll be here much longer," Mrs. Downey said as Peter turned around and walked away without going back in the room for his hat.

Peter didn't know what he had done wrong. He was disappointed that Jennifer felt uneasy about him. When Peter got home, he looked in the bathroom mirror wondering if he wasn't as good-looking as he once felt he was. He initially didn't want to go back to the group anymore but felt there may have been other people who felt more positive towards him. Tears started to come down his eyes as he realized he needed a job. His choice was either to find work or move back with his parents. He could see no other options at that present time.

Chapter 18

Peter called his mother the next morning, but she didn't answer her phone. She was busy working a double shift that day. Peter went online to look up Sarah, the girl he liked when he was much younger, on Facebook. He had previously tried to avoid looking her up because he was afraid of the possibility that she had found a romantic partner. She now lived in Portland, Oregon according to the information he discovered in her online profile. She still had braided hair. Peter sent her a friend request hoping she would recall who he was.

In a matter of minutes, Sarah accepted his request. There were no questions asked. Peter was afraid to send her a private message but looked through her profile. It appeared that she worked at a local supermarket. She lived with her family, both her mom and her dad, who were in some of the pictures she had posted on her page.

Two days passed since the friend request was sent. Peter was getting nowhere with the resumes he had sent out to prospective employers. He decided to write Sarah a private message confessing that he once thought she was amazing and that he wanted to know things such as what she liked to do in her spare time. Sarah quickly responded.

Hi. Got your message. Thanks. I actually do remember you from school, but we hardly knew each other. I don't think that you'd find me "amazing" if you really knew me, especially now. I'm really quite ordinary. Sorry to disappoint you. Anyway, we live so far away from each other now. It'll be nice having you as a friend on Facebook. Thanks for the add.

Peter felt compelled to write something back to try to let her know she was amazing in his eyes but thought that, perhaps, she'd find that odd. He didn't want to scare her off and was grateful that he added her as a friend on Facebook and could follow whatever posts she would decide to put up.

With nowhere else to go the following Wednesday, he decided to show up at the church's young adult group and give it another try. Maybe he could at least get his hat back.

Mrs. Downey was seated in the room before anybody got there. Peter showed up and she said "hello" to him.

"Hi. Did anybody turn in a baseball cap last week? I left my hat here last Wednesday."

"Yes. It's over there on the coat rack," Mrs. Downey said as she pointed over to the other side of the room.

"I was actually hoping to see you early. In fact, that's why I got here earlier than usual," Mrs. Downey continued.

"Why did you want to see me?"

"I talked with Father Matthew yesterday and he knows a Catholic high school in Queens that's hiring someone for their admissions office."

"How did you know that I have office experience?"

"I remember you brought it up when you first came to the group, and Father actually looked your profile up on Linkedin."

"That was nice of you guys."

"Yes. If you're interested, the school's principal would like to meet you. Are you interested?"

"Of course, I am. Where is the school?"

"It's in Jamaica."

"Not too far."

"Not at all."

"If you want me to call Father Matthew, he can set up the appointment for you tomorrow afternoon," Mrs. Downey continued.

"That would be amazing."

"Do you want to stay for tonight's group or get ready for the interview tomorrow?"

"Are you sure I'll be able to interview tomorrow?"

"Positive. They're desperate for someone to help sort the student files and put the paper files' information from years back onto the computer."

"Well, I guess I'll go home and prepare then."

"I'll have Father Matthew call you in the morning and give you all the information."

"Thanks. Thanks so much," Peter said as he put his baseball cap on and exited the room.

As the young adult group members started walking in, Peter was on his way out of the building and wondered why nobody asked him why he was leaving. He didn't care about the fact nobody spoke to him from the group as he was more excited about the job Mrs. Downey had mentioned to him. As soon as he got home, Peter called his mom. She answered the call on the third ring.

"Hi, Mom."

"Hi, dear. I saw you called earlier. Is everything OK?"

"Things just got better. I have a job interview at a high school tomorrow."

"That's absolutely wonderful, honey. See. I told you things would work out if you were just patient."

"They'll be working out, I guess, as long as I get the job."

"How did you get the job? Through an ad online?"

"Actually, I got it through the church."

"That's great. There's probably less competition then."

"You're right. I never thought about that," Peter said.

"Should I tell your father or wait until you get the job?"

"Maybe you should wait. I don't want to get his hopes up too much until I see what it pays."

"Hopefully, it pays close to what you were making before."

"I guess I'll know tomorrow. I'll call you tomorrow night."

"Sounds good, angel. Talk to you then."

"Goodnight."

Peter received a phone call from Father Matthew the next day as he was promised. Peter learned the school was quite a prestigious one and that he would have a lot of responsibilities if he accepted the position. Father Matthew told him that the salary would be discussed on the interview which would occur at 3 PM later that Thursday afternoon.

Peter was excited as he took out a nice button-down shirt and ironed it while trying to figure out how to loop his tie correctly. When he was ready to leave his apartment at 1:45 PM, he gave himself one last glance in his bathroom mirror before heading out to the interview with the school's principal, Mr. Keebler which would start promptly at 3.

Chapter 19

When he arrived at the high school, Peter noticed the students were all dressed well and looked very studious to him. He was hoping he would get the job and be able to catch up on his bills. This school he was interviewing with was once an all-boys school but was changed over to co-ed some years back. As he entered the school, the security guard gave him clearance to walk towards the principal's office. Peter proceeded to sit down in the waiting room after announcing his presence to the secretary.

Mr. Keebler was sixty-one years old and had a little more than two years left before he planned to retire. He saw Peter waiting and walked over to introduce himself.

"Peter, it's a pleasure to meet you," Mr. Keebler said extending his hand out to him.

"It's an honor," Peter replied as he shook his hand.

"What happened at your last job?" Mr. Keebler asked during the middle of the interview which had been going quite well.

"Well, my job got switched over to a non-paid internship. There were budget cuts."

"Budget cuts are all too familiar to us these days. With student enrollment at an all-time low, I have to have three different temps sometimes coming in every week but if you want the job, I'd be happy to offer it to you, so we don't have to see a different person in the office every day. It would be nice to have a familiar face here again in this role.

"I'd love to work here."

"I'm glad we heard about you. I wasn't sure we'd ever fill this position. The salary is about five thousand less per year than you were making at your last job. I have to let you know that."

"That's better than I had hoped for and I really feel comfortable here. The commute isn't too bad either."

"So, if that's a "yes," give Suzy over there your ID and SS card, and you can start as quickly as tomorrow. Does that work?"

"Yes, yes it does."

Mr. Keebler and Peter had a good interview together and seemed to get along pretty well. The principal left Peter with Suzy who was the school's administrative supervisor. Suzy was 46-years old and had a kind persona which made Peter feel instantly comfortable.

When Peter told his parents the good news about getting the job, they were so happy for him. Megan offered to come see him over the weekend since she had a day off that upcoming Saturday.

"Can Dad come too?"

"Your father has to work overtime. But I could come over and maybe we could go out to eat dinner or something. It would be nice to see you. I'm so proud of you for getting the job."

"It wasn't too hard. I just needed the connection which I got through the church."

"I knew you'd find something. I'm really happy you signed up with that church. Sometimes, prayers get answered if you just keep believing."

"I've had a few thoughts about my faith, recently but I guess I'm back on speaking terms with God after today."

"God is always there when you need him the most."

"I guess. Saturday night sounds good. I'll see you then. What time is good?"

"How does three in the afternoon work?"

"Sure, that would be great. See you at 3."

Peter started his new job the next day and found time moved quite fast as he was filing documents and learning the school's procedures. Suzy was helpful and answered his questions whenever he had a problem come up. Peter found the job to be fairly easy and straightforward. He had a good first day.

At lunchtime, in the employee cafeteria, he had seen a few of the teachers sitting there and some were close to his age. Peter believed he had the potential to make friends with one or two of them and hoped that this would be the perfect job for him.

Chapter 20

Andrea, John's officer from Heaven, was looking down on Peter hoping that he would meet someone in the next few years to marry. Peter still had a tremendous shyness much like the one John had possessed. Andrea was glad she managed to give John a new life although he had forgotten about his past life while his soul inhabited the body of Peter. God called on Andrea for a meeting about some concerns he had regarding Peter's insecurities.

As Andrea was seated in her office, she addressed God's concerns.

"He is doing much better at this point in his life than John was," Andrea said.

"We can't give everybody a second chance. This was a real gift you gave John."

"I know. John had it hard. His life was cut shorter than it should have been."

"What's the point of sending him back to Earth, though?"

"I think he would have been bitter as an angel here in Heaven."

"He's a good worker. I think his strengths lie more in vocational skills than in relationships. I'm not sure Peter will be able to have a thriving relationship at this point. We're more than halfway through the time we gave him. He has to start making good soon to fulfill the agreement that was made."

"He will. I have a feeling. Now that's he's setting down the foundation for his career, the rest will follow. You just wait and see."

"I hope you're right Andrea. My worst nightmare is that he comes back here, and we have another bitter soul on our hands. Do you know what I'm saying?"

"He was never truly bitter. His life had been cut short. That would have made anyone bitter although I think that's the wrong word to use. I think, this time, we're giving him a more well-rounded opportunity to make a prosperous life for himself."

"Let's hope he makes good decisions."

"I'm hoping he does."

"Let's pray for Peter."

"I have a couple of intakes coming up. I have to start getting their files ready so we can welcome them."

"Please do. You're a good officer. We'll look back in on Peter after a few more months."

"There is one other issue I wanted to discuss with you, though. John's sister, Meredith, is going to be diagnosed with advanced breast cancer. Her time on Earth is coming to an end. Is there any chance we could have Peter see her before her time is up in seven months?"

"That's a good idea. They won't know each other but it would be nice to let them have a moment together. Wouldn't it? How could we orchestrate it?"

"Can't we give Meredith a little more time?"

"It's cancer. It's really out of our control. We can't extend her life anymore. I think fate should intervene. Give Peter's parents a chance to win tickets to Disneyland in California. Meredith should find a reason to go to Disneyland too. That's where they're best to cross paths."

"How can we ensure they'll meet?"

"You know there's never a sure thing, but I'll work my magic and see what we can accomplish."

"I hope we can extend closure to Meredith regarding John before she dies. She always felt John's death was her fault."

"It was never her fault. We'll do what we can. I'll start working on it. Go take those incoming spirits right now, OK, Andrea?"

"Yes. I'm on it."

Chapter 21

Meredith's husband, Richard, had recently died of a heart attack. Meredith still lived in California and was determined to get in touch with her son, Jason and her daughter, Allison, who she had seen a few weeks ago at Richard's funeral. Both kids were in their early 30's. Jason was working as a criminal attorney in Chicago while Allison was a soon to be married librarian at a library in New York City. Meredith, who was retired, had felt lonely lately and was going to the doctor soon to get medical tests done. She dialed the number of her son, one Saturday afternoon.

"Hi Jason," she said when he answered the phone.

"Hi, Mom."

"I was thinking of you. I wanted to thank you for helping pay the funeral costs for your dad."

"Of course, Mom. I didn't want you to have pay those bills all by yourself."

"I wanted to see if maybe you and your sister wanted to get together in a month. I wanted to plan for a day out. Maybe we could go to Disneyland."

"Sure, one weekend, I'll fly out there and we'll go. Just call Allison and see if she's good to go too. I don't know her schedule. I can pay for her plane ticket, no problem."

"Aren't you busy at work these days?"

"Of course, why do you ask?"

"You said 'yes' to me awfully quickly. These days, it seems like you take my calls more than you used to before your dad died."

"I guess I've woken up to reality. I lost my dad without spending enough time together and I don't want the same thing to happen with you."

"Thank you. You don't know how good it feels to hear your voice after all I've been through these past couple of months."

"I love you, Mom. Call Allison. See how she's doing with her fiancée, Stephen."

"I hear Stephen's doing good. He teaches at a school for the deaf. I know he loves her and I'm so happy for them. I can't wait until they finalize plans for the wedding."

"It'll be fun. A wedding is just what this family needs. It was so nice of him to propose at Chelsea piers. Allison always loved that place."

"I'll call Allison now. Maybe we set something up for next month. I'll let you know when Allison tells me availability."

"Sounds good, Mom."

Meredith smiled after the call although she felt that her health was deteriorating. She didn't know if anything was wrong other than old age but wasn't sure she'd see the wedding Allison would have with Stephen. Meredith wanted to organize a get-together with her children soon just in case she was sick. She had always loved her children and was feeling the void of Richard's absence a lot these days.

Meredith wanted to make the most of the time she had left. She had always missed John and wished he could have still been alive so she could talk to him about life. They used to have conversations as children about movies and life that she had fond memories of. One such conversation was had when John asked her how she ranked the Harry Potter movies. Although, the answer of how she ranked them fascinated John more than herself, Meredith always felt comfort in knowing how much John really cared about which film she had truly enjoyed the most. John had always had that sincerity that she admired him for so much.

Meredith called Allison. She picked up the phone after one ring.

"I'm working, Mom."

"How much longer until you get out?"

"I'll be home in about an hour."

"Can I just ask you one thing?"

"Sure. What?"

"Do you think you could get off sometime next month for a weekend to come see me and your brother? We talked about going to Disneyland here in California."

"Definitely. I've got two weeks paid time off left and I'm sure Stephen would be into that. Call me later, and we'll talk. Maybe I could stay a week or something."

"Sounds good, dear. I'll talk to you soon."

"I love you, Mom. Bye."

Chapter 22

At work, Peter found that he managed his time extraordinarily well. Sometimes, he would be so ahead on projects he was working on that he found out he was way ahead of schedule. This efficiency allowed him time to check in with his mother, Megan, whether she was on lunch break or off from work depending on the particular day Peter called her. His dad, on the other hand, wasn't allowed to take calls at work since his job was so full of high pressure. Josh was stressed out a lot lately and had conveyed this to Peter during a recent phone call they were on together.

One day, Megan had helped treat a patient from California who worked at Disneyland and this patient offered a discount on tickets to the theme park. She called Peter to see if he would be interested in taking a few days off work to fly out West and go to Disneyland.

"You got cheap tickets, Mom?" Peter asked.

"They were incredibly reasonable."

"What about Dad?"

"I'll work my magic on him. You're in, right?"

"After all the troubles I've had the past several months, I would love to take a few days and just unwind," Peter said.

Megan thought it would be a great idea for the family to go to California and she encouraged Peter's dad, Josh, to utilize some of his precious vacation time which he rarely used.

"This is just what you need, Josh," Megan said right after he agreed to take some needed time off from work.

"I haven't been on a vacation in forever," Josh said.

"We can spend some quality time with Peter," Megan reminded Josh.

"Is that what Peter wants?"

"Yes, I spoke to him about it and he's ecstatic about finally clearing his head for once."

About a month had passed when Peter, Megan, and Josh found themselves on a plane heading to California. They had a hotel stay planned at Disneyland and were going to stay there for three days and four nights.

When they arrived at their hotel, Peter felt he needed a few minutes to unwind in the hotel room before the three of them embarked on a mission to see all the different aspects of the theme park. Josh and Megan went downstairs to eat lunch at a restaurant on the first floor of the hotel while Peter blasted the air conditioning and sat on the bed. He needed at least an hour to relax after the long morning airplane ride they had taken to get there.

Meredith and Allison were walking down the hallway of the same hotel Peter and his family were in. They were going to get ice while Jason and Stephen were back in their own hotel room. As they walked silently down the hall of the third floor, Peter who was wearing a New York Mets baseball cap came out of his room to get some ice himself. When Peter opened the door, it accidentally hit the side of Meredith's arm.

"I'm sorry about that."

"It's OK," Meredith said as she stopped and felt her arm.

"Are you in pain, Mom?" Allison asked.

"No, you should look before you open the door, young man," Meredith told Peter.

"I didn't know anyone was there. I was closing my eyes almost asleep before I decide to get some ice. I was on a long plane ride from New York."

"You're from New York?" Allison asked him.

"Yes."

"What part?" Meredith asked as her arm started to feel a little better.

"I'm in Queens but my parents live on Long Island."

Meredith continued, "I'm from New York too. Where did you grow up?"

"Mostly on Long Island."

Meredith asked him, "Are you parents here with you?"

"They're eating a late lunch downstairs."

"Don't ask him a million questions, Mom," Allison said.

"I know. I apologize. Just watch when you open doors next time," Meredith reminded Peter.

"I will."

"Well see you around maybe," Allison said as she continued over to the ice machine with her mother.

"See you around," Peter said as he walked with his bucket over to the ice machine.

After Allison filled a bucket with ice, Peter proceeded to go ahead and fill his up. Peter thought Allison was quite attractive and hoped he would see her again during the next few days.

Peter sat on his hotel room's bed after pouring himself a nice glass of ice water. He took his hat off and wiped sweat from his forehead with a towel. He was ready in a few more minutes to go down and meet his parents to take a tour of Disneyland and hopefully see some sights he had never seen before.

After two days of going on some of the lighter rides, and seeing some attractions, Peter was ready to leave soon. He had seen enough Disney characters to satisfy his appetite. Peter also grew tired of having expensive lunches and dinners some of which Peter helped pay for. While his parents went out for a romantic dinner one night, Peter headed back to the hotel room. On his way there, he saw Allison again only this time she was in the hallway fighting with Stephen. Peter went in his room but pressed his ear against the door to hear why Allison was arguing with her boyfriend.

"We're finally able to do something nice for my Mom. Why can't you understand how important this is to me?"

"I know that. There's a lot of problems at work and I really shouldn't have taken the week off," Stephen told her.

"You don't know how long my mom could have left. Dad died and you know how close I was to him. Can't you just pretend to be happy?"

"Why couldn't we just commute here instead of staying three nights in a hotel?"

"It's what my mother wanted. She didn't want to cook, clean or deal with anything like that for three nights. Can't we just give her what she wants?"

"I guess," Stephen said before apologizing to Allison about complaining to her.

Chapter 23

When Peter, Megan and Josh were seated at their last dinner in a California restaurant, Peter noticed Meredith sitting alone across the way at a table for one.

"That lady over there is on our floor. I bumped into her by accident the other day," Peter told his parents.

"Let's see if she wants some company," Megan said.

Peter got up and walked over to Meredith. He gently waved hello to her before talking.

"Hi. My parents are here. Remember me? The guy from New York who hit your arm."

"Yes. I remember."

"Are you alone?"

"My son is a lawyer working on a case upstairs and my daughter had to work some things out with her fiancée so, yeah. I'm alone."

"Come join us at our table, then," Peter said.

"That's not a bad idea. Maybe we could talk about New York," Meredith said as she took her glass of wine and walked over to the waiter to ask him if she could join Peter and his parents at their table.

When the waiter confirmed it was OK, Meredith sat down, and Peter introduced his parents to her. Meredith explained how she was originally from New York as well.

"New York. The city where you work around the clock and still can't pay your bills," Josh jokingly said.

Meredith continued speaking.

"I left New York a long time ago. I do miss it sometimes. I have actually lived here in California for so many years now. I think it was definitely the right choice to leave, though."

"So, no regrets?" Megan asked.

"None whatsoever," Meredith replied.

"You live in California. Why did you want to come to Disney and stay in a hotel if you live so close by?" Josh asked.

"I'm from San Francisco. It's not really super close. I just wanted to get an overload of Mickey Mouse and friends to help me cope with my husband's recent death. I'm with my kids. I needed to cheer myself up and they're good kids."

"I'm so sorry about your husband," Peter said.

"What do you do, Peter?"

"I work as an assistant for a Catholic high school in Queens."

"That's great."

"I'm a nurse," Megan said,

"Do you want to know what I do?" Josh asked.

"It's OK," Meredith said as she started to talk to Megan about the makeup she was wearing and they both realized they were wearing the same brand of lipstick.

"I love you, Dad," Peter said as he looked over to Josh as the two ladies were discussing their shoes and what places they shop at.

"You remind me so much of my brother when he was young," Meredith told Peter towards the end of their dinner together.

"Why is that?"

"I don't know. Just the way you present yourself. Do you want to see a picture of me and my brother when were young, just about your age?"

"Sure," Peter said.

Meredith showed him a picture of her and John when they were both in their 20's. Peter took a glance at the slightly torn picture and felt a little peculiar in seeing how much John seemed to resemble him. Peter noticed striking features which were similar, namely the eyebrows and nose.

"Did John come along too? Maybe we could meet him," Josh said.

"Oh, he's long gone. He passed away more than 20 years ago."

"I'm so sorry for your loss," Peter said.

"It's OK. It's been a while."

"What was he like?"

"A little confused but he had a gentle soul and a good heart," Meredith said.

"Sorry for asking. I was just curious," Peter said.

"It's no problem at all. I'm so glad you bumped into my arm in the hallway that day. I had a great time tonight talking to you guys," Meredith said as she saw Allison and Stephen coming into the restaurant to get her. Although Meredith offered to pay for her meal, Josh insisted to let him put it on their bill instead.

When it came time for Peter, Megan and Josh to leave for the airport the next afternoon, Peter decided to knock on Meredith's hotel room door to say "goodbye." Allison opened the door and told him she was sleeping and that she'd let her know he said "goodbye."

After Peter thanked her and walked away, Allison wished him well on his return to New York. Peter smiled as he got on the elevator to exit the hotel with his parents.

Chapter 24

On the plane ride back, Peter was resting with his head back on the seat as his parents were both reading. Peter was thinking of the photo he had seen of Meredith's deceased brother, John. Peter felt an inexplicable attachment to the man in the photo and wished he could explain why he felt like he had a connection to John. In any event, he was glad he made a friend in Meredith and thought he could even look her up on Facebook being that he knew her name and that she was from San Francisco.

When Meredith checked out of the hotel, she felt this would, perhaps, be the last vacation she would be going on in her lifetime. At one point, she was almost totally out of breath during the trip in the car back home, and she knew she was getting older. Her kids were busy in the car on the way home. Her son was texting a client while her daughter and her fiancée were talking about planning their wedding that Meredith hoped she would attend one day.

Meredith had felt a connection to Peter that helped bring back memories of her brother John who she missed immensely. She hoped one day, she would see John and talk with him the way she used to when they were kids. Meredith knew her time on Earth would soon be up by the way she had been feeling lately and was using the time when she returned home to tie up loose ends regarding her finances. She hoped to be greeted in the afterlife by her husband Richard who had meant so much to her.

Meredith pulled pictures of John and her parents out of an old photo album one afternoon while she was alone in her living room. John was on little league in some of the pictures while in others he was seen playing basketball. John played poorly and wasn't good at any particular sport. He found his passion in the movies and Meredith viewed pictures of their father with them at an old Steven Spielberg movie from the 1980's. Meredith could remember it being a perfect day for her, John and their father.

She had severe chest pain as she realized she was alone in her home and that her kids were back living their lives again. When the pain lessened, she took out a sheet of paper and started to write letters to her kids that she would place in a box when she finished writing them. Meredith hoped her kids would find them one day and know how much she truly loved them.

In a dream later that night, Meredith was visited by John who put his arms around her.

"It was never your fault," John told her as Meredith started to cry and hugged him back.

Meredith thought of Peter and wondered why fate let her meet him. Maybe, this encounter was just God's way of letting her know that John was going to be OK since they looked so much alike. She didn't have to know the true reason for Peter and his family entering her life. She was happy. She was also content in knowing that John seemed to have found peace if the dream she had that night was any indication.

While Peter slept that night, he found himself waking up in the middle of the night crying. He was upset he had to go back to work and saddened that his parents were back on Long Island. He missed them a lot. Then, he thought of

Meredith's face and smile. She seemed so content to him even though she had lost her husband. He decided to follow her example and let go of what he thought he wanted in life and accepted what he had as he fell back into a deep sleep with only two hours left before he had to get up for work.

Chapter 25

It was a few months later when Peter looked up Meredith on the internet. He had been busy with work and was trying to find a girlfriend on dating websites in his free time. Peter found Meredith's profile on Facebook and learned that she had been diagnosed with cancer. He wanted to say something and reach out to her. However, when he thought harder, he believed that everything he had experienced by meeting her meant so much to him. He didn't want to extend his sympathies to her now and remind her that he time on Earth was running out. From the online pictures, it seemed her family was with her and that she was enjoying her last days the best she could. He even learned online that Meredith did, indeed, attend her daughter Allison's wedding.

Peter found that his job offered him the escape from reality he needed. One day in the high school employee cafeteria, he started talking in depth to Joseph who was 31 years old. Joseph was one of the history teachers at the high school.

"You seem to like it here," Joseph said.

"What makes you say that?"

"Well, you seem like you know the place like the back of your hand. You make your coffee and sit in here looking like the happiest guy to be on lunch break," Joseph continued.

"I've learned to make the most of my life and what I do."

"You can be an inspiration to some of us teachers."

"It's simple, really. I love what I do. It means the world to me and I cherish every day I'm here at work."

"It's great to have that kind of positivity."

"I always try to be a positive person."

"Have you thought about teaching?"

"I never completed my degree. I thought about it one day."

"Well, it's something to think about. Hey, I have to head to my next class. Talk to you tomorrow, same time, same place?"

"Sounds good. I'll be here."

When tomorrow arrived, Joseph and Peter found out that they had a lot of similar interests such as writing poetry and watching television.

"I wanted to be an English teacher and a poet but I knew I couldn't make a living doing it, so I majored in U.S. history," Joseph said.

"That's cool. I love writing. I could write for hours on end," Peter said.

"What do you write about?"

"About God mostly. I've written a few poems myself about the dreams I have. The ones that I can remember at least."

"I've written a few short stories, myself. I've thought about taking a night course in English and sharpen my skills just in case a position opens up here."

"That's a great idea."

Joseph became Peter's work buddy and they shared conversation every day on their lunch break. Eventually, they met for lunch one Saturday afternoon at a café in Queens and had discussions about women.

"I'm still single, actually," Joseph said.

"I hope I'm not single when I'm your age."

"You're almost here at this age, buddy. You're just a handful of years away. What are you looking for in a girl?"

"I'm looking for someone who gets me. It's not easy finding someone who understands me."

"Well, you seem pretty easy to get along with. I get you and I think you'll find someone if you keep trying. Do you go to bars?"

"Not really."

"Do you have an online dating profile?"

"I took it down."

"Why?"

"I want to meet someone the old-fashioned way."

"Well, the old-fashioned way is tough nowadays."

"Do you have an online dating profile?"

"Four of them, actually. I just have them on paid sites. I get nervous a student's parents or, perhaps, a friend could see my profiles online and change their opinion of me. I have to be careful. I'm a role model for the students, you know?"

"I see. Well, that makes sense to me."

Peter and Joseph ended up seeing a movie later that night. They found themselves looking at pretty girls who were passing by them in the theater on their way to sit down. While the movie they saw was just decent, they enjoyed spending time together and agreed to see each other at work on Monday.

When Sunday came, Peter went to mass and saw people from the youth group present at the mass. He hadn't been attending groups anymore and it hardly seemed like anyone from Wednesday nights remembered him. When he saw

Jennifer from the group, and tried to wave to her, she didn't look his way at all, let alone notice the gesture.

Chapter 26

Peter found himself online one night after speaking to a girl from a dating site on the telephone. Their conversation did not go well, and he found himself explaining why he was religious to a girl who had no religious affiliation herself.

Peter then started looking at an adult website he found in passing which offered female "escorts" for home delivery. While he was afraid of bringing one into his home, he thought of the idea of meeting one in person at a local motel. He was tired of being lonely and not experiencing sexual pleasure. Even Joseph had admitted in their conversations that he had been intimate with some of his past girlfriends. Peter felt like he was the only one not having sex although he wasn't 100% sure these escorts would, indeed, have sex with him.

When he called the escort agency, he asked what "type" of girls they had available.

"We have all types, honey, what are you looking for?"

"Perhaps, a girl in her 20's with dark hair and eyes."

"We have plenty of girls like that. I have Mary, a 20 -year-old girl with nice long brown hair and brown eyes, 110 lbs. and 5'2."

"How much?"

"$200 for Queens residents."

"Thank you," he said as hung up the phone.

He did not feel it was moral to have an escort come to his home or meet one at a hotel. His religion played a major factor in his decision to hang up the phone. He did make an agreement with himself that he would try the "escort" idea if he didn't meet a female that he liked by the time he turned 30.

Lately, Peter's dreams were quite interesting to him. He tried writing things down about what he had dreamt when he woke up every morning especially when visions of God appeared in his dreams. These visions included some conversations that seemed to revolve around topics of life. Peter didn't tell his friend, Joseph, about the dreams because he was afraid of looking like a religious "fanatic" to him. However, Peter was determined to write down information on conversations he would have with God in his sleep.

One morning, Peter made an entry in a journal he had created regarding what he believed he had dreamt the night before.

God came to me last night and asked me why I don't try harder to find a nice girl to settle down with. He told me I was "morally obscure" by considering sex with a stranger and looking at pornographic sites. I asked God how he knew about the time I visited a pornographic website and he informed me that, as God, he knows all. Then, another female figure appeared in my vision before I woke up and realized I had to get up for work.

Peter soon realized how hard it would be for him to wait until the age of 30 to have sex. He wanted to find someone he loved but felt awkward trying to be around women. While he was more comfortable around his friend, Joseph, he realized he didn't have the desire to be with a man sexually although that would never happen as Joseph had admitted to him that he was "straight" in casual conversations.

When Peter decided to explore online escort advertisements online, he came across one girl who was supposedly 24-years old, thin, and had long dark hair. Her face was blocked out of the pictures she had posted online but she had an apartment in Queens that she accepted her "clients" in. When he called to find out the cost, he discovered it was about a third of his weekly paycheck (after taxes) to see this woman for a half hour.

Although Peter didn't pursue seeing this woman who called herself "Tara" online, he kept her in the back of his mind just in case he got lonely enough to decide to "see" her.

Chapter 27

At work, Peter made the most of his days and although his job became mundane in terms of the tasks he was assigned, he was always kept busy. Eventually, Joseph's teaching schedule changed for the new school year, and new teachers came into the employee cafeteria where Peter ate lunch. Peter didn't connect as easily with any of the new teachers as he did with Joseph.

After six months passed, Peter looked for "Tara" online to see about meeting with her in person. He couldn't wait any more time to experience the companionship of a woman. Recently, he had been rejected by a girl named Anne. He asked her out in the cafeteria at work. She was a new teacher who was a few years younger than him. She told him that he wasn't her type when he offered to take her to dinner. Embarrassed, Peter started to find himself in the computer lab at work on his lunch break instead of the cafeteria. Luckily, the computer teacher, Mr. Jeffries, liked Peter and was happy to let him sit in the lab.

When Peter called Tara, he set up an appointment with her on a telephone call to go over to her place which was about a 10-minute train ride from where he lived. Not knowing the right thing to do in this situation, he stopped off at a local florist and purchased a single red rose to give Tara. Then, he went to the ATM to take cash out to pay Tara for her time.

Tara directed Peter to her apartment while talking to him on the telephone when he arrived at her address. She opened the door as he got to her apartment on the third floor of the building in which she lived. Peter was fascinated by her glamorous look although she looked at least 30-years old. He noticed she was wearing heavy makeup and lipstick but believed she was quite attractive.

When Tara closed the door after letting Peter in, she took the rose from him and asked for the money.

"Thanks for the flower. Do you have the money?"

"Sure. Here you go," Peter said as he took two hundred dollar bills out of his back pocket.

"Leave it on the dresser," she said as she started to get undressed.

Peter felt sleazy after he undressed himself as she told him to. He felt that what he was doing was sacrilegious and immoral. However, he had sexual desires that had gone unfulfilled for many years which he wanted to experiment with.

Tara took a wrapped condom from a bowl on the nightstand and used her teeth to open it. She noticed Peter only had a slight erection and was going to use her skills to make him more comfortable and become more stimulated.

"Put your head back and relax," Tara said.

While Tara started performing oral sex on him, he asked her what her real name was.

"I don't give my real name. Just call me Tara," she said.

"It feels so good," Peter said as she continued pleasuring him.

Peter opened his eyes and caressed her long hair until he felt so aroused that he needed to stop her before he ejaculated. He pushed her head up.

"That was so great," Peter said.

"Don't you want to fuck me?"

"OK."

"Do you want me on top or do you want missionary?"

"I'll take missionary, I suppose."

"You suppose. How sweet?"

Tara sat back on the bed and closed her eyes as he got on top of her. She was waiting to feel him penetrate her, but he was nervous and didn't know how to put himself inside.

"Can you help?"

"Sure, baby. Give me your dick," she said as she reached down.

"Push it in," she continued to say.

Peter started moving it forward deeper until he had fully penetrated her. He felt so weird. It was almost like the whole world was watching him have sexual intercourse.

After a few thrusts, Peter ejaculated. Tara asked him to keep having sex with her. He kept pushing it in more until he felt like the condom was no longer on. He looked down and it had fallen off.

"Thank you, baby," she said as grabbed the condom in a tissue and threw it out.

"What do you like to do for fun," Peter asked as he started putting his clothes back on.

"I like getting my hair done, my nails, movies, nothing crazy."

"Well. I think you're gorgeous."

"Thanks for the compliment."

"Can I see you again, sometime?"

"Call me. I'll save your number, so I know it's you."

"I had a great time. I'd love to see you again."

"I work every day except Wednesday. I have class that night."

"What kind of class?"

"You ask a lot of questions. It's just a GED class."

"I see."

"I can't do this forever."

"Are you really 24?"

"No. Sorry to disappoint you, baby. I have a client coming up in a few minutes. It was nice to meet you."

"Nice to meet you too," Peter said as he exited her apartment door and walked back downstairs and left the building.

Peter felt like he did something wrong. He didn't know how to accept what he had just done. In the moments as he was walking away, he felt that he would like to get to know who Tara really was, discover her real name and possibly date her. Maybe then he would feel less ashamed at what he had done.

Chapter 28

In the days after his experience with "Tara," he started getting nervous. He was hoping that nobody would ever discover what he did, but he knew if he had a real-life partner one day, he would have to tell her he had sex with a total stranger. He believed in honesty. Peter felt disgusted and even thought of telling the priest at his church in a confession about what he had done with this woman. Although confessions are supposed to be confidential, Peter feared of the priest sharing his secret with another person in the church. He was also scared of Father Matthew finding out since it was with his help that he had obtained his current job.

Peter started fumbling with the papers he was filing at work one day. Suzy, who was supervising him, was concerned.

"What's bothering you Peter?"

"Nothing, Suzy," he responded feeling paranoid that she knew something about his sexual encounter.

"You seem nervous. Just relax. I know employee reviews are coming up. You've done quite well since you started. I'm pretty sure you'll get a good review. There's no raise this year, unfortunately."

"I'm not worried about the money. I just feel happy I have the job."

"What's the problem, then? I see you shaking."

"There's no problem. Maybe I just need a drink of water," Peter said as he went over the water cooler and filled a cup with water for him to drink.

Peter took a deep breath and told Suzy he was feeling better. Suzy went back to analyzing school records on her computer. Peter sat down in the corner of the office alphabetizing paper files for the students who were coming in next semester. He felt at ease and came to terms with the fact that probably nobody would discover his sexual experience and he was determined to keep it a secret.

When Peter arrived home, he deleted his online personal ads that were posted to certain dating sites. He wanted to save money to see Tara again next month so he could see if there was any potential for them to get to know each other outside of sexual intercourse. He was intrigued by her and felt that if she was doing what she was doing, she must have felt some insecurity in her life.

As the days went on, however, Peter started to feel guilty regarding what he had done with Tara. He felt as if he violated his religion by have pre-marital sex and, in doing it with someone he didn't know, he was ashamed of himself. What he had done was definitely something he didn't believe he could talk comfortably about with his parents. When he wasn't working, he felt nervous. He was not nervous about a friend, faculty or family member finding out about his encounter. Instead, Peter was afraid God knew what he had done and would never forgive him.

Peter turned to Joseph and, although he didn't reveal exactly what he had done, Peter explained why he was feeling guilty. Peter and Joseph were talking about what Peter felt on a telephone call.

"I disobeyed a commandment," Peter said.

"What commandment did you disobey?" Joseph asked.

"Thou shall not have premarital sex."

"I don't know if that's a commandment per se."

"It is. Isn't it?"

"The church frowns on premarital sex but I don't think you've broken a commandment or that's what you've done is unforgiveable."

"You've had premarital sex, right?"

"Yes. I've had a few relationships in which sex played a major role."

"If you weren't in a relationship, would you have done it, though?"

"Probably not. Who did you have sex with?"

"I can't talk about it."

"Why not?"

"I don't want to talk about it."

"Is it someone at work?"

"No. That's all I'll say. I wouldn't jeopardize my job by doing something so stupid as have sex with someone from the school."

"Good. Because I was afraid you were going to say you did something with a student."

"Never."

"Thank God. You just seemed so nervous. How am I to know if you don't give me all the details?"

"Thanks for talking to me, Joseph. It means a lot. I'll have to figure things out for myself. We should see a movie sometime. Maybe next weekend I'll give you a call."

"Sounds good, buddy. Stay positive and remember one thing."

"What's that."

"It's just sex. OK?"

"OK. Talk to you soon."

"Goodbye."

Peter's religion was important to him. He didn't know how to adequately fulfill his sexual desires and what he had done led him to believe he "sold out" to the devil. Peter thought about abandoning his religion and that things would never be the same for him because of his mistake. However, God was too strong a presence in his life. He had to get through this hurdle and make his life work for him somehow. If he could learn from his mistakes, maybe he could pick up the pieces of his life and put them together again.

He thought a lot about Tara and hoped maybe by turning the sexual encounter into a relationship of some sort that God would forgive him for what he had done. He put away a little money each week so he could see her again. It would be a way of saving himself if he could do something nice for Tara even if they couldn't be in a relationship of any kind. Whatever would happen with Tara, Peter wanted to know. He wanted to know more about the girl he had sex with.

Chapter 29

Andrea looked down on Peter from Heaven. She was discussing Peter's situation with God.

"This guy can't get anything right. No matter how hard he tries, he keeps messing up, "Andrea told God.

"He's a really nice guy. I can't even believe his guilty conscience is getting the best of him like this. He lives in New York. People from New York are usually a lot less conscientious."

"That's a huge generalization. Don't you think?"

"C'mon, Andrea. We call what we see. I don't think it's labelling the people of New York by saying they usually break the rules without so much as blinking an eye."

"That's so unfair to New Yorkers."

"It's justified. Let's stop arguing. I see all. I know all. Peter is a rare case. I truly hope he makes the best out of the next 10 years or else I don't know what we can do."

"We'll have no choice but to take his soul back."

"Patience, though, Andrea. I like this guy. I want to see where he's going with things. In fact, I'll try to speak with him in his dreams a little more. Perhaps, steer him away from his negativity."

"All you can do is try. I have faith."

"Of course, you have faith, Andrea. You've seen almost as much as I have."

"Thanks, but you know that's not true."

"You have seen a lot, though. Let's see what Peter does. We'll discuss his case again in a few weeks."

God and Andrea were staring down at Peter on Earth as they saw him setting up another appointment with Tara that Saturday afternoon.

"Tara. I want to see you."

"Sure, what time?"

"In about an hour," Peter said.

"No problem, baby."

When Tara opened the door upon Peter's arrival, she looked a little frustrated. Peter wondered why she seemed so distressed as she was pouting as he handed her the money for their session.

"You seem a little down today," Peter said.

"I'm happy. I could really use the money today. I have a lot of bills I'm behind on."

"Maybe I could cheer you up a little."

"I love having sex so you'll make me feel better. Don't worry, baby."

"I was wondering if I could take you out afterwards."

"I don't date clients."

"Don't see me as a client then. See me as a friend."

"But you're a client."

"That's not fair."

"I don't date anymore."

"What if I paid you for the date?"

"$200 an hour to take me out?"

"I could take you out for an hour. Do you take PayPal?"

"I guess I could take PayPal. Where do you want to take me?"

"Maybe out to lunch. There's a diner down the block."

"I've never been to that place. That's not a bad idea."

"Should we do this first?"

"Yes, let's get this over with, first," Tara said as she opened up a condom.

Peter felt awkward when she put the condom on him. He wanted to be her friend and get to know her, but he was about to have sex with her again. He felt a little conflicted until Tara started performing oral sex on him. His eyes opened wider as he felt intense satisfaction.

After the act was over, Peter asked Tara if she wanted him to send her the money electronically for their date.

"Sure, send it over, now. I'm going to get ready. I'll be in the shower."

"OK," Peter said as she started getting ready.

Peter had to split the payment between two different credit cards in order to finance the date. He also had to have at least $50 in available credit to pay for the food at the diner which they were going to have on their date. It seemed so expensive, and he felt irresponsible, but he liked Tara and wanted to do the right thing even if he wasn't sure what the right thing to do was.

Chapter 30

As they were walking to the diner together, Peter admired out of the corner of his left eye her beautiful long hair. He even liked the old-fashioned leather jacket she was wearing.

"Where did you get the jacket?"

"One of my clients gave it to me. I had told him my coat had gotten a cigarette burn in it, so he brought me over his ex-girlfriend's leather jacket which she had left in his closet when they broke up."

"That was nice of him. It looks cute on you."

"Listen. When we get the diner, please be careful what you say. When the hour's up, I'll let you know. I'll be discreet about it. Please don't mention money, OK?"

"You're actually timing the hour?"

"I might give you a few extra minutes. It depends how fast our waitress is and if I want to get dessert."

"I see. Well, be as accommodating as you can. I spent almost a week's salary today," Peter said.

"You don't have to tell me how much you make. I appreciate it."

"I didn't want to say that. It just came out. I really like you. I just want to do right by you."

'What do you mean?"

"We've shared a couple of great times together. I just don't want you to think I'm only after one thing."

"It's OK if you are only after one thing, though."

"I'm not, though, and this date should prove that."

"It does. Thanks for taking me out. I haven't been on a date in a few weeks."

"Why not?"

"Most guys want a slam, bam, thank you, ma'am. They don't want to talk too much. Do you know what I mean?"

"I want to talk to you. I want to know what makes you who you are. I think you're a kind, compassionate woman. And, on top of that, you're also really pretty."

"Thanks for the kind words. We're here, so let's pretend we met on a dating site or something like that," Tara said as they arrived at the diner.

"Let's talk about TV shows, our families, things like that."

"Sounds good. We met on Match.com, OK?"

"Sounds perfect," Peter said as he opened the front door of the diner and Tara stepped in front of him to walk in.

While they were looking at their menus, Peter began to speak to her regarding his food preferences that afternoon.

"I prefer to have a hamburger. I'm a simple guy."

"Well, I don't want to put you out too much money. Maybe I'll just get a cheeseburger then."

"Please, don't worry. Get what you want. Well, I'll just get a small cup of chicken noodle soup and a cheeseburger. That'll make me happy."

After they ordered their food, Peter glanced over to Tara's wallet which she had put on the table after taking out some chap stick which she put on her lips. He saw her ID visible in the front cover of the wallet and discovered Tara's real name was Teresa.

"Teresa without an "H," eh?"

"Peter, how did you know that?"

"I just saw it on your ID."

"Damn it. I forgot to put my wallet back."

"Don't tell anyone my name, OK?"

"Of course, not. It's just between you and me."

"Thanks. I can't believe I messed up. Nobody knows my real name."

"Well, I know it but I won't use it against you so just relax."

"Why would you use my name against me?"

"I don't know. Why don't you just tell people you're close to your real name?"

"I hate my name."

"Why is that?"

"It sounds so religious."

"It's a beautiful name."

"Try to erase it from your memory. I'm Tara," she said.

When the waitress came over with the soup, Peter smiled and sat back in his seat. As he watched her eat her soup, he thought she looked really sweet. She looked so innocent that he could hardly believe what she was doing for a living.

"This soup is delicious," she stated.

"It looks yummy."

"Do you want to try a noodle?"

"No. Finish up. I'm saving room for my burger."

"So, what do you do again, Peter?"

"I work for a high school."

"Do you teach?"

"No. I just do office work."

"I think I did office work in a past life and really hated it. Because I had gotten a job as a secretary a few years ago, and only lasted two weeks."

"Why do you think that is?"

"It's so boring to just sit in the same office all day long."

"I can relate to that. There aren't enough people coming through as far as my office is concerned. I only see other people when I get to the cafeteria for lunch. Well, I see the people I work with in the office, but they become like furniture. They're just in the background. You hardly notice them. If it weren't for everybody getting excited when the principal asks someone to do something, then I think I'd be so bored at my job."

"What do you think you were in your last life?"

"I don't know. I'm not sure I believe in reincarnation."

"Well, what religion are you?"

"I'm Catholic."

"I guess you don't then. I don't really have a religion. I grew up with a Jewish mom and a dad who didn't care that much for religion."

"You know what's funny, though."

"What?"

"When I was in California not too long ago, I met this lady and she showed me a picture of her dead brother. I swear if I didn't believe people could be born again."

"What do you mean?"

"He looked so much like me."

"It's possible you, know."

"What is?"

"To come back in another body after you die."

"I don't know. I'd like to believe I'm living my life, and this is my one life to live. YOLO as the expression goes. You only live once."

"Where did you hear that expression?"

"In school. The students like to say it," Peter said as the waitress left their burgers on the table.

"I don't believe that we only live once. I believe we come back again and again especially if we mess up. We keep going until we get our life right."

"That's a nice way to think. I want to get my life right this time, though."

"Well, the one way to try to get it right is to find someone nice, don't you think?"

"I found someone nice. You."

"I mean someone nice who is on your level."

"I think you're on my level."

"I know. I think you're a cool guy but how could we have a future?"

"Why couldn't we?"

"You work at a school and I have my job."

"You won't be working your job forever. You can get a better job."

"For what? Minimum wage? I can't live on that little money."

"You could try if you found someone you truly loved."

"I guess. I think I'll keep my options open just in case I meet someone," she said as she was chewing her burger.

Peter felt so hurt that she wasn't seeing him as a potential romantic partner, but he started to feel a connection to her in regard to some of the things she had been saying about coming back in another body after death. He had a lot of thoughts about that subject and wanted to talk to her about them in more detail the next time he saw her.

"I will schedule another date with you when I get the money," Peter said.

"Why would you go out with me again when you know we'd never work as a couple?"

"Well, number one, I'm convinced we could work as a couple and number two, I think you're interesting. I like getting to know you."

"I'm so flattered," but time's running out for today."

"Oh, man. Just my luck."

"I'd try to get you to pay again but I know you don't have the money."

"You're right. You're definitely right about that."

"Keep me in mind but I'd rather you save your money for someone else. Maybe a regular girl. Perhaps, somebody you work with. You're a great guy. Any girl would be lucky to have you."

As she got up from the table and put her coat on, Peter started to feel his heart break again. It was yet another girl who was making him feel hopeless. Only this time, he believed that this particular girl had posed a challenge to him that he was ready to take on. That challenge was to try to be the best man for her. He knew it wouldn't happen overnight, but he wasn't ready to give up. Not quite yet.

Chapter 31

When Peter spoke to his parents again, he told them everything was going "really well" at work. He didn't have long conversations with his parents these days as he was more interested in thinking about Teresa with his free time. At work, he used his lunch break to volunteer at the high school library where he checked out books for students. He managed to bring his lunch with him to the library and ate it while volunteering five days a week. He felt safer in the library than in the cafeteria. He didn't want to get in any conversations with the staff that would put his job in jeopardy, so the library was the perfect place for him to spend his lunch break.

In about a month, Peter had saved enough money to see Teresa again. He called her up and made an appointment for 2 PM on a lonely Saturday. When he walked up to the apartment and Teresa opened her door, she looked even more beautiful to him than she did the first time he met her. Peter was happy as she invited him in and asked him if he wanted a drink of water.

"That would be great," Peter told her.

"I'm happy to see you again. We're fooling around here, not going to the diner today, right?"

"That's right," Peter said.

"Did you miss me?"

"Yes. I did. Why do you ask?"

"I've thought about you recently. I wondered if you would call again."

"You have my number. You could have called or texted me."

"That's not the way it works in this business. How do I know that you didn't meet a nice girl and get engaged in the past month?"

"I think you know that couldn't happen so quickly."

"I'm not so sure with you. You're awfully spontaneous. I see a troublemaker in you."

"A troublemaker?"

"You look like you would do anything to find the right girl."

"Maybe you're right."

"Well, get undressed, and sit down on the bed," Teresa said as she took her T-shirt off followed by her bra.

"I'm so happy to be here."

"I know you're happy. You already told me that," she said as she gave him a quick kiss on the lips.

"I wanted to know about your dreams."

"My dreams?"

"Yes. What do you dream about? Do you ever dream about your past life?"

"Who said I had a past life? Oh, you mean the conversation we had at the diner, right?"

"Yes, you remember it, don't you?"

"Vaguely. I mean, yes, I dream," she said as she started kissing his penis which was covered by a condom.

"Maybe you could tell me your dreams."

"My dream right now is for you leave the $200 on the dresser. I should have collected it already."

"I don't have it," Peter said."

"What? I started sucking you off. You bastard."

"Just kidding. I have it," he said as he pulled 10 twenty dollar bills out of the right pocket of his pants which were on the floor.

"Oh. Thank God. I'm sorry. It's just that I don't usually start doing anything until I collect my money and I trusted you. Thank you, baby," she said as she glanced over as he placed the money on the dresser.

"Is it all just about the money with you?"

"Look. I'm going to be honest. I don't work for myself. I have to give the money to my pimp before I get my cut."

"Your pimp?"

"Yes. I tell him my appointments, and he watches the guys as they enter the building from an apartment across the street. He knew you already, but I usually text him when I get the money. I told him I trusted you."

"Did you text him the day we went to the diner? Yeah. When you weren't looking at me."

"So, what does "having a pimp" mean, exactly?"

"He gets a cut of what I make and makes sure the police stay off me if he can help it. I just wanted to let you know. Don't mess with his money. Ever."

"I wouldn't do that."

"I know," she said as she continued sucking on his erect penis.

After they had sex, Peter asked if she could tell him a little about her dreams regarding her past life.

"Give me an extra $20 in case we run into some overtime. At least I can tell my pimp you tipped me."

"Sure. Luckily, I saved a twenty," Peter said as he handed her the money.

"I dream that sometimes I was Marilyn Monroe in my past life. I had an affair with President Kennedy."

"Really?"

"I don't know. I mean I feel I was a blonde who looked like her in one of my past lives and I lived a very ritzy lifestyle. That's what I'm trying to recapture now."

"You think having sex with strangers will help you recapture a past life that was so glitzy?"

"I don't know. It's a start."

"What were you in your dream or your past life?"

"I was a movie star."

"Well. It's really hard to be a movie star these days."

"Why is it so hard?"

"You have to memorize dialogue and be in front of live audiences and television cameras."

"I want that life. At least, I think I do, sometimes. I'd never have to worry about money again."

"I just want to live a normal life, myself. Last question: Do you ever have conversations with God in your dreams?"

"No. I don't think God and I have such a close relationship, if you know what I mean."

"I get it. OK. We'll talk more next time I muster up more disposable income."

"How romantic?"

"I'm sorry. Wait a minute. Didn't you say at the diner that we keep going in life until we find the perfect life."

"Yes. Someone was listening, I see."

"Wouldn't being Marilyn Monroe be the perfect life? How could it get any better than that?"

"It could get better. Life can get better for anyone. Remember she died when she was fairly young. Maybe I'm supposed to live the full life she never lived."

"I see. Anyway, I didn't know you had a pimp. It sort of makes running away with you almost impossible. You're making what I was hoping to happen pretty much unobtainable."

"I know. I feel bad. Sorry to disappoint you. If it's any consolation, if I weren't doing this job, we'd probably have never met at all. I hope we can still see each other again."

"We will. Thanks again," Peter said as she let him out of the apartment.

As Peter walked away, he was upset with himself for believing of possibilities that would probably never happen in any sort of reality. However, he was still determined to keep seeing Teresa just because she intrigued him in ways he had never been intrigued before.

Chapter 32

Back at work, Peter occasionally lost focus on what he was doing while thinking about Teresa and what she was doing as well as who she was doing it with. He felt sorry for her even though he knew she didn't seem to mind what she was doing that much. He wished he could know the whole story about her life and felt he probably never would learn all the things about her he felt compelled to know about.

Peter was still having unusual visions at night which included conversations with God about topics Peter could hardly remember when he woke up the next morning. He did remember a little bit and the latest entry in his journal read as follows:

Last night, in my dreams, God was asking me why I would have sex with a woman who had multiple partners and did not love me. I told him I felt like this woman was very special and that I could save her from the path she was following in her life. Then, I saw an angel in Heaven come to me and let me know I had to control my desires if I wished to be granted entrance into Heaven. That's where it all gets a little murky. I know God was telling me what I was doing wrong in life and scolding me but everything became a blur when I woke up and realized I had overslept ten minutes and was close to missing the bus I usually take to work.

As Peter attended Sunday mass and received the Eucharist, he felt like he needed to confess his sins to a priest regarding the premarital sex he had with Teresa. It all made him feel so dirty inside despite his feelings of admiration for Teresa. He thought about her a lot, but he wanted to try to move on for a little while. He wasn't eliminating the possibility of seeing her again, but he wanted something, perhaps, a little better for himself.

On the next night Peter had a dream that he remembered, it was completely different from the dreams he was used to having. He yearned to talk to his mother about it but when he called her to try to get her opinion, she was busy doing laundry. He glanced over his most recent journal entry which read as follows:

Last night, I dreamt of going back to school and trying to enroll in college again. In the dream, people were making fun of me in school because of my age. I turned out to be naked in the dream and didn't know if that was the real reason that they were laughing at me. I was so embarrassed when I woke up. I wonder what would happen if I went to college again as a 30-year-old man. Would people really make fun of me? I know, with my job, I couldn't make nighttime classes at the college unless I took them online. This dream really opened me up to the possibility.

Thinking that college could open up the door to better dating possibilities for him as well as better jobs, Peter looked at his local four-year city college's requirement to gain admittance. He didn't want to obtain a reference from an old teacher, and he didn't want to pay the $75 application fee. He also couldn't transfer over his coursework in which he received less than a 'C' from his old college. Peter believed it may have been too late for him to go through college at this point. He had to make this current life work for him so that meant that he should try to see what other jobs were out there and begin dating respectable girls from the online dating sites. Those things, he believed, would lead to his happiness.

Surprisingly, for him, he got a response through a dating site from a seemingly nice girl who worked at a local bank. She was a little overweight and wore big glasses, but he believed she was quite cute and attractive. When they spoke on the phone to set up an in-person meeting, Peter enjoyed listening to her soft voice. Her name was Eleanor.

"So, you work at a high school?"

"Yes. I'll tell you which one when we meet."

"You can tell me now. I promise I won't tell anyone."

"When we meet would be better. I just am using a little caution in case we don't get along or something."

"Why wouldn't we get along?"

"I don't know. Blind date and all."

"We've seen each other's pictures."

"It's just that we have to see if there's chemistry, no?"

"OK. I get that. We'll see what happens when we meet then."

"Do you pray a lot? I read in your profile that you believe in God and that everything happens for a reason."

"I pray sometimes. Not as much as I probably should. I think God knows I love Him."

"I think he knows. I guess we can talk about our faith when we meet."

'Sure. What do you like to watch on TV?"

As Peter and Eleanor discussed shows they liked on Netflix, Hulu and other channels, Peter felt a connection and was looking forward to meeting her. He set up a date with her which included a show and, possibly, a potential invite back to his apartment. He said they could get dessert and bring it back with them if they felt "comfortable enough."

At work the day before his date with Eleanor, Peter received a text message from Teresa. It read:

Can we get together? I'll take a few bucks off for you. I really need the help.

Peter didn't have enough to pay Teresa and take Eleanor on a respectable date, so he declined to answer the message. He really wanted to help Teresa but there wasn't enough money in his bank account to do so. If he paid Teresa even $50 then he believed it would interfere with him making a good impression on his date.

He received one other text message from Teresa that day which was simply a question mark. Peter ignored that one as well. He took a bus to the Queens mall to buy a shirt for the date that was coming up with Eleanor. He selected a beige button-down collared shirt which was a little nicer than the ones he wore to work. Luckily, for him, it was reasonably priced at $14.99.

Chapter 33

Peter had agreed to meet Eleanor in Manhattan for a Broadway show. She had purchased tickets for the play at $30 a ticket and Peter had the money to reimburse her for his ticket. While waiting for her to arrive, he checked his phone and saw no new messages from anyone on it. His Facebook account had mostly work friends from his job and they weren't communicating much with him these days outside of the high school. He had told his father about the date he was going on and both his dad and his mom were excited for him.

About a half hour before the show started, he received a text message from Eleanor that stated she was running late. She apologized that she was going to be "a little tardy." Peter didn't have a ticket to go in to the show alone so he patiently waited for Eleanor to arrive. As the time passed, the show began, and the ticket taker at the theater announced that they would not be letting anybody in again until after the intermission. Disappointed, Peter still believed Eleanor would show up and he hoped they'd see the second half of the production together.

Eleanor didn't pick up her telephone when he tried to call her. While he was waiting, Peter was very anxious, and he didn't know how to handle the situation. He thought about getting on a train and going back home but he didn't want to disappoint Eleanor in case she had run in to an emergency and still showed up to meet him.

It became clear as her phone went straight to voice mail that she wasn't answering his phone calls. Peter believed maybe her phone battery had died. He didn't know, for sure, what had happened. He didn't want to go home so early that night especially without meeting Eleanor, but he boarded a train back to his apartment wondering what had happened to her.

Peter got home and took his new shirt off. He was hoping to hear from Eleanor, but he wasn't happy that she didn't arrive for their first date. If something had happened, he would have understood and he wondered what could have happened that would have prevented her from calling him and letting him know she would be a no-show.

As Peter went in his bed to go to sleep, his phone vibrated with a text message:

Sorry, you're not my type. Take care, Peter.

Peter began to think about the time he had been waiting for her and wondered if she had seen him waiting in front of the theater and left. It all felt very disappointing to him. He wanted to call Eleanor to get more information but figured she said everything that needed to be said in the text message that she sent him.

Instead of going to mass the next day, he decided to stay in and sleep until noon. It was the first Sunday mass he had missed in a while. As the days passed, he thought of Teresa. Hating himself for ignoring her, he didn't have the courage to call her back again. How could he explain that he ignored her when she seemed to have needed his help?

After work one day, Father Matthew texted Peter.

Hi, Peter. It's Father Matthew. How's it going? I hear you're doing a good job at the high school. Are you enjoying the job? I wanted to get ahold of you at mass last Sunday, but I didn't see you there. Text me back.

After reading the text message, Peter realized that he had to hold himself up better emotionally. There was a lot that keeping his job depended on such as going to mass and making appearances at school functions. He had to show people he really cared about the job and that it wasn't simply a means to make money for him. Peter's values, within himself, had seemed to have changed since he started the job, and he knew it. However, he replied back to Father Matthew with positivity.

Everything's great! Thanks for checking in. I went to mass on Long Island with my parents this past weekend. I'll be back at church next Sunday. I love the job. See you soon.

Chapter 34

During the time that he slept, Peter found the most interesting things in his life happened. They happened in his dreams. In his most recent dream, he found himself on a beach with Teresa walking on the sand together with beautiful imagery dominating the backgrounds of his vision. He hadn't been to the beach since he was 15. He felt tremendous guilt regarding ignoring Teresa and wished that God would come to him in his sleep and tell him what to do. Since God didn't "speak" to him in his recent dreams, he wondered if he could find a way to get the answers that he was seeking at the next Sunday mass that was coming up.

At the next Sunday mass Peter attended, Father Matthew was the priest. During his homily, Father Matthew discussed the meaning of and effectiveness of perseverance in the life of a good Catholic.

"A good Catholic must be determined to go after what he or she wants in life and do everything possible to reach his or her goals in life. With God by a person's side, a devout Catholic must never be afraid of the devil. The devil is among us, almost at all given times, in one shape or form or another. Sometimes, it takes the strength and determination of a good Catholic to shun the devil. Whether it be to support one's family such as doing a good job at one's place of employment or taking care of one's children emotionally, we must never forget the power of perseverance," Father Matthew explained.

As Peter listened to Father Matthew speak, he felt somewhat inspired although Peter believed he was quite ambitious, himself, and that he pursued his desires quite aggressively and frequently. Peter understood the concept of being tempted by the devil all too well. Peter always tried to do the right thing in his life. While he understood, Father Matthew's speech, Peter also believed in the concepts of rejection and failure which Father Matthew seemed to oversimplify in the homily.

When Peter took a train out to visit his parents after mass, they picked him up at the Long Island Railroad train station by their home. Peter's dad, Josh, was seated in the front passenger seat and began to ask his son a personal question.

"Peter, have you met anyone nice recently? Perhaps a nice female to introduce to me and your mother? Maybe a nice girl to help carry on the family name?"

"Not yet, Dad. I'm always trying. These dating sites are so difficult to use.":

"Why are they difficult to use?"

"Well, Dad. There seems to be a lot of spammers out there. I would assume so since I hardly get any true responses when I have an ad up. Everybody seems to have a gimmick. Maybe I'm just not that good looking. That could be it. In fact, I think that is it."

"Don't say that about yourself," Megan told Peter.

"I haven't thought about the real reason. I'm just not meeting anyone. I just don't take dating lightly because the whole concept just makes me feel insecure. All that rejection, especially."

"I see," Josh said.

"It's just that all our friends who have kids your age, well, it seems like they're either getting married or having kids. We just want that for you too. Maybe if you had a girlfriend, you'd be a lot happier," Megan added.

"Maybe. I don't know, Mom."

Megan cooked Josh and Peter a nice steak dinner that evening and they had a fun time together as they started to play a movie trivia game Megan had ordered for Peter online. While his parents knew few of the answers, Peter excelled at answering many of the more difficult questions in the game. Peter knew what won for Best Picture of 1981 at the Academy Awards even though that film came out way before he was born. It was released almost 40 years before he was born.

On the train ride home, Peter thought about why he seemed to know more about certain topics than others and wondered why he was so bad with women. He felt cursed, at times, and at others, believed he may have had a higher calling in life. Maybe that calling was to help Teresa. He didn't know, for sure, but he was determined to try to see if he could pick up the pieces from not calling her that time she had asked for his help.

Peter was frustrated when he got home. He knew he had to prepare mentally for work the next day and for the week ahead. His job became like a routine and he was growing tired of it. He wanted to start his life over again with a new job but since he remembered how hard it was to actually get a new job, he started thinking of what he had as more of a blessing than anything else.

Chapter 35

When he slept the next few nights, his dreams had become hard to decipher. A lot of things seemed to happen in them that didn't make sense. When he would wake up, he'd have no recollection of anything sometimes and, as a result, wrote nothing in his journal those particular days.

Andrea and God looked down at Peter. They were thinking that he may have been a lost cause. Sometimes, Andrea believed they should have let John move on to the next place in the afterlife.

"We should have let John go on to the next chapter after life. He may have been happier up here."

"He had a lot to answer for, Andrea. There's no guarantee he would have made it to a good place up here. He'd always been selfish in certain ways, and now Peter is displaying some of those selfish tendencies. Do you know what I'm talking about?"

"Is he selfish because he never gives anything to himself and always does what is expected of him? I'm not quite sure what you mean."

"You know as well as I know that if he lowered his standards and just dated an average girl and if he accepted his place in society that he would flourish."

"Flourish?"

"He'd find some level of happiness. The type of happiness that I hope every human being and even every animal can attain down there on Earth."

"It's a big world down there. Anyone can get lost trying to make sense of it. John and Peter are both the same man. Erasing his memory of the past doesn't erase who he truly is."

"I feel this was a mistake then."

"His life was taken early. That's the real reason we gave him another chance. Everybody deserves a fair amount of time on Earth to discover happiness," Andrea said.

"In a perfect world, yes. But this world is anything but perfect. We know that Peter strives for goodness. He even wants to help Teresa, who frankly I believe, is not able to be saved no matter what."

"Don't you believe in all your children down there?"

"I do. Of course, I do. I wish some of them would resist the passions of the flesh and just learn to adapt to living a normal life."

"Normal is no longer easy to define in the world. Human beings have changed the definition of what normal is through free will and their personal achievements in life."

"You're right about that. Peter's going to have 10 years to prove himself. That is, if Teresa, has the baby."

"What do you mean?"

"Well, it's Peter's baby she's pregnant with. If she does have the baby, then all Peter would need to do would be to get married. He'd technically already have the family if the baby was born."

"Even if they're not together?"

"Well, they're not going to get together now. We're going to have to see what happens over the years and if they find each other again."

"Do you really think Teresa would try to raise the baby alone? That's why she called Peter that day. She'll never know the baby is his, but she wanted his advice as to what she should do with the baby."

"Let's hope for the best for these two."

"I, realistically, only see these two as potential soul mates so far. Let's see what Peter does next. There's always hope we can try to steer him on another path."

"Through dreams?"

"You know what we do up here. Better than anyone else, you know," Andrea said.

Chapter 36

Several years passed, and today, Peter turned 33-years old. On the morning of his birthday, he was told his hours at the high school would be reduced to 25 per week which meant he would have to enroll in the lower priced medical insurance plan. Losing 15 work hours seemed like it was going to be hard on him financially although Peter was optimistic at the prospect of having more free time. He had some interest in trying to explore other career opportunities that were available.

As a gift to himself for his birthday, he purchased a three-month long membership to an expensive online dating website. This site had more advanced "matching tools" that would supposedly help him locate his ideal match more efficiently.

Although his parents had invited him to their home for dinner that night, he decided he would rather celebrate with them the following Sunday instead. Peter hadn't used a dating website for several years and the prospect of using one had never seemed better for him than now. He had become more lonely than usual and was ready to meet someone nice to settle down with as per his parents' wishes.

Peter came across a profile of a 28-year-old woman who worked in the medical profession. He liked her approach to online dating. She was offering a reply to every single person who answered her ad. Her name was Tracey. Peter wrote her a response detailing his interests, what he did for a living and the type of girl he was looking for. He stated he was looking for a girl who was honest, above all else.

Tracey promised to answer all those who replied to her, and she answered his message in a matter of minutes. She didn't seem at all thrilled with the prospect of dating Peter. He felt puzzled as he read her response.

I'm looking for someone who makes a little better of a living for himself. Thanks anyway and good luck to you, Peter.

Peter was quite upset. Having outgrown the age requirement for the young adult group that met at his church, he believed online dating was his only hope of meeting someone compatible with him. It was with great trepidation that he went on an escort website to see if he could find someone who was more likely to have sex with him than the girls on the dating site.

He didn't want to take risks again by meeting another prostitute, but he came across a 26-year old's "adult profile" who seemed amazing to him. She was very attractive to Peter. She called herself "Candy." She seemed like an intellectual type to him as he viewed her online picture which was taken in a library. She was wearing glasses in the photo. He found out through a text message the cost of seeing her was $200. Peter didn't have the money readily available but took a cash advance from his credit card and headed over to see her at the designated address she texted him.

Candy provided him with the address of a motel and Peter was concerned of this fact when he arrived in front of the place. He was ready to turn around and go back to the train station to head home when he received a phone call from Candy.

"Are you almost here?"

"You didn't tell me you were in a motel."

"Don't worry. It's all safe," Candy said.

Peter walked up the stairs to the second floor of the Queens motel where she had promised to be staying. When he got to her room, a slightly older woman opened the door and invited him in.

He walked in the motel room when the lady, who looked nothing like "Candy" did on the website, asked him to undress and leave the "donation" on the bed.

"Where's Candy?"

"I'll get her for you if you leave the donation on the bed."

"Sure," he said as he stripped down to his underwear and left the money on the pillow.

"Thank you, baby," the woman said as she started taking her top off.

"Where's Candy?"

"I'm Candy, baby."

"Do you like my tits?"

"They're nice," Peter said as he realized something more may have been going on than he had originally anticipated.

"You can touch them for another $100."

"It's OK," Peter said as he got up from the bed and started to put his clothes on.

"Where do you think you're going?"

"It's OK. I'm sorry to bother you."

This woman then walked in front of him and asked him for more money.

"You can fuck me for $300."

"I just gave you $200."

"Nobody leaves this room without paying $500."

"I don't have that kind of money," Peter said.

"I'll ring downstairs if you walk out the door and tell the owner you raped me."

"What are you talking about?"

"Pay me the money."

"I don't have any more cash."

"There's an ATM in the lobby."

"I don't have the money."

"I'm going to sit here for a minute. You're going to find out a way to get me another $300 or I'll call the cops and tell them you raped me."

"They would need proof."

"Look in the garbage pail over there," she said.

When he looked, he saw a used condom in the garbage pail. He was frightened and thought of calling his parents and asking for help. That would embarrass him since he declined an invite to their house that night.

"What do I have to do to get out of here?"

"Give me three hundred more."

"I have three credit cards. I could take $100 off each. I have no money in the bank at all."

"Do what you have to do but get me the money," she said.

Peter got dressed. She walked with him out to the lobby where Peter proceeded to take three separate $100 withdrawals from the ATM. Nobody was in the lobby except the guy who worked there who was sitting behind a window minding his own business.

When Peter handed her the money, she told him to "get lost."

Peter was shaken up by this event and was scared. He didn't know what had just happened but was surprised he had actually been so stupid. What had happened those years back with Teresa had made him think paying for sex was easy even though it was not something he did in his life that he was proud of.

Now, he would have to ask his parents for money to get through to the date of his next paycheck. He had always been self-sufficient since he left their home. He was ready for the embarrassment to follow for what he had just done.

Chapter 37

Peter successfully borrowed two hundred dollars from his mother which she sent him through PayPal. He told her that he had gambled the money away on lottery tickets to avoid telling her the truth. He had learned a hard and expensive lesson, but he felt that maybe meeting someone through any ad was a bad idea. He left his profile on the dating site for three months but obtained no responses to it during that time.

Although Peter believed in God, he had given in to temptations that he felt were strongly against the religion he was practicing. However, he had to go to church every Sunday in order to make an appearance for Father Matthew to see he was still practicing Catholicism. Although his job had cut his hours significantly, he wanted to do the right thing. He was scared to confess his sins to a priest for if word ever got out to anyone in the parish, he would most likely be deemed, at the bare minimum, a sinner.

Whenever Peter would let go of the ideals of Catholicism to pursue his dreams of love and intimacy, he felt lost. It was too late for him to go back and erase anything that he had done. He wanted to start over and was hoping that God would give him another chance to prove himself worthy of his religion.

There were no groups for people his age to attend at his church except for Bingo. However, he had to promise his mother never to gamble again at the time she lent him the $200. He didn't want to get caught up with gambling even if he were to keep it a secret from his family. Peter knew if he wasn't careful that more trouble would ensue especially if he lied to one of his parents again.

Peter discovered he had more important things to worry about later in the week. He received a call from his mother, Megan, when he got home from work one evening.

"Your father had a heart attack."

"What, Mom?"

"Your father's in the hospital. He had a heart attack on his way home from work."

"Oh, no. I'm so sorry. Can I go to the hospital?"

"You should try to come tomorrow right after work if they don't release him tomorrow. I can meet you at the railroad and take you there."

"What about tonight?"

"I don't want to pressure you. It's almost 7:00."

"Don't worry. What time do visitors' hours end? I could try to get a cab or something."

"Save your money. Visitor's hours end at 9. They may release him tomorrow if he gets better. We just have to wait and see."

"What do you think happened?"

"He's been under a lot of stress lately. He's getting too old to be working these long hours he's been putting in, you know?"

"I figured it would catch up to him. I know he wanted to try to pay off the mortgage."

"I don't want to hear about money anymore. Health is much more important. I'm here at the hospital now. He's sleeping. The doctors are going to call me later or in the morning with an update. I'm heading home in about an hour. I have to go to work, myself."

"Is he in the same hospital where you work?"

"No. It's about a half hour away. I've got to get changed and eat dinner."

"Why don't you take off?"

"I can't. I just hope I get through the night."

"You will, Mom. Don't worry. Everything is going to be alright."

"I hope you're right."

"It will all be fine. Dad's a fighter."

"You're right about that. OK. Good night, Peter."

"Good night, Mom."

Peter started praying again and asked God to watch over his father, Josh. Peter rarely prayed out loud before but that night, he did.

I know I've been really stupid, lately. I've abandoned my faith, at times, but now I am starting to see the big picture, God. I realize I've been more concerned with getting laid or with watching television than with my own family. Maybe, I'm stupid and it took my father ending up in the hospital for me to realize what an asshole I've become. Please don't let anything happen to my father. Please, God. I'll do anything. I'll confess my sins if I have to. Just keep him alive for Mom. And for me. Keep my dad alive so I can visit more and show him I'm not a failure. He needs to know that. Thank you, God. In the name of the father and of the son and of the Holy spirit. Amen.

When tomorrow came, Josh was still in the hospital although they were just keeping him for observation. It seemed like he was going to get better soon though the doctor prescribed two medications for Josh to start taking. Also, the doctor recommended Josh cut his workload down significantly. That's when Peter decided to offer to move back home with parents. Megan knew they would need help financially and agreed that Peter coming home would offer them a little financial security if he could help with just a few hundred dollars a month in expenses. Megan didn't even want to think about potential medical bills for the hospital stay.

Peter charged a $500 move of his basic furniture and possessions to his credit card. He was happy to be moving out since he was only working 5 hours a day. When Josh saw Peter for the first time after getting out of the hospital, he was so happy. Having Peter back home, Josh and Megan felt something they had missing for a long time: A sense of family.

Over their first dinner together as a family since Josh's release from the hospital, Peter realized he liked having dinner with people every night of the week. He especially loved having dinner with his own family. Peter had been lost but now he found himself again.

Being with his family made Peter feel less inclined to do stupid things and he even went back to online dating again dealing with a different group of girls than he did in the city. Now, he would get to see what it was like to talk to Long Island girls. Peter was looking forward to getting to know what type of girls lived out on the Island and how they compared to the city girls he spoke to. Josh even agreed to lend Peter his car if he ever wanted to use it for a date.

Chapter 38

Peter eventually set up a date with a girl named Alicia. She was 30 years old. Alicia worked at a veterinarian's office in Lynbrook. Out of the three women Peter spoke to on the phone since moving back home, Alicia sounded the most compassionate out of all of them. She loved animals and was honest which he believed was her best quality. She had a caring personality.

When Peter did the math to realize how much he would need to finance the date with Alicia, he felt lucky he was only paying a few hundred a month rent to his parents rather than the almost $1000 a month price tag that his former apartment had. He was taking Alicia out to a chain restaurant to get something basic like hamburgers with her. They were looking forward more to dessert than the meal itself. They both seemed to have a passion for junk food.

Megan had taken Josh's car to get gas while Peter was preparing for his date with Alicia one Saturday evening. Peter was ironing his shirt and getting himself ready by combing his hair afterwards.

Megan brought the car home to Peter with a full tank of gas so he could pick Alicia up in style. Megan didn't want her son showing up on a date using the railroad. In fact, she believed Peter should use the extra money he was saving to drive places on the Island. She wanted him to think about getting a used car for himself.

Peter thanked his parents for letting them use the car. Both of his parents wished him "luck" as he headed out to his date with Alicia.

When Peter arrived at Alicia's house, he called her to announce his presence outside. She told him to come to the door and to ring the bell. After ringing the doorbell, Peter was nervous and heard a man's voice say he was coming to the door.

Alicia's dad, Kenny, answered and invited Peter into the house.

"How are you doing, young man?"

"I'm not sure I'm so young anymore, sir."

"You two kids are babies still."

"That's reassuring to know. I feel like life's running away from me sometimes. Running rather quickly."

"It can feel like that sometimes," Kenny said as he asked Peter to take a seat on the sofa in the living room.

"Where's Alicia?"

"She's still putting on her makeup and doing her hair."

"I'm not putting on my makeup. I'm just picking out shoes!" Alicia screamed from upstairs.

"Women," Kenny said.

Peter laughed as Alicia started making her way downstairs and into the living room. When Peter saw her, he was quite happy. She looked sweet to Peter as he got up from the couch to shake her hand. Alicia had her hair in a bun and both her fingernails and toenails were painted dark red. She had black shoes with a small heel on the bottom of them. Alicia was almost as tall as Peter with her shoes on.

"Where are you two going?"

"We're just going to Chili's."

"That sounds like fun. What is it that you do again, Peter?"

"I work for a high school. I do administrative work for them."

"That sounds good. I'm glad you do something. Well, you two have a good night out. I'll wait up for you. OK, Alicia?"

"OK, Dad."

Peter opened the car door for Alicia to get in. As she got in the passenger seat, he started feeling the joys of knowing what a real date felt like. Alicia may not have been the prettiest girl he'd ever met but she was real and sincere. He was happy to be living a more normal life for once.

At Chili's, they both ordered specialty lemonades. Peter was inspired by her choice for a mango lemonade and decided on having a strawberry one, himself.

"Where do you see yourself in, I don't know, say a year, Peter?"

"I would like to see myself secure in either my job now with more responsibilities or a new job that pays a little more."

"What about romantically? Where do you see yourself romantically?"

"Well, I'm not getting any younger. I would like to see a relationship blossom with somebody special."

"I feel the same way," she said as she took a sip of her lemonade.

As their eyes glanced towards one another, Peter smiled but then started to feel guilty about his past. He didn't ever want to confess his previous sexual experiences with Teresa to Alicia. He didn't want her to know what he had done in order to experience sexual satisfaction.

Alicia was laughing in the middle of their dinner together as Peter shared a story about how a kid at the high school came to be known as "Plastic Man."

"This kid, whose name was Henry, wore plastic bags on his expensive Nike shoes whenever there was rain outside or snow or anything or that sort. Hail, whatever, All the teenage girls thought he was cute, and this one girl called him "Plastic Man" and the name stuck. So, Henry started wearing plastic bags as gloves and a plastic bag over his head as a hat. He wore earmuffs in the winter too, made out of-you guessed it-plastic bags. The girls thought he was a gem and he had like four dates lined up on the prom. I don't know which one he picked."

"That's really funny," Alicia said as the time had come for them to order dessert.

While scooping up pieces of a chocolate chip cookie covered with ice cream together, they started feeling a bond developing. Peter and Alicia's honesty towards each other that night was something that both of them appreciated quite a bit. While Peter didn't disclose a lot of information about his personal life, the details that he chose to reveal to Alicia were all the truth.

When it came time to drop Alicia off, Peter wanted to walk her to the door, but he saw Kenny looking out the window and decided just to say "goodnight" to her. Alicia kissed him on the cheek and when she did, Peter smelled the beautiful perfume she had on which was a flowery scent that really aroused his senses. Peter wanted to kiss her back, but she had already stepped out of the car and was heading over to the house where Kenny had just opened the door for her.

Peter was happy. He was ready to tell his parents he had a great date. As he was driving back home, he thought that maybe a new beginning was ahead for him and that, perhaps, Alicia would be the right girl for him. He didn't know, for sure, but he felt satisfied with life again. He was truly joyous for the first time in a while.

Chapter 39

Peter had exchanged text messages with Alicia the next couple of days. Things seemed optimistic in terms of a second date happening for them in the not-too-distant future. One day at work, Father Matthew showed up unexpectedly and asked Peter if he could speak with him in private. Peter agreed and the two of them went out to the hallway to discuss what Father Matthew had on his mind.

"I haven't seen you at mass, recently, Peter."

"I know. I had to move back with my parents on Long Island since my hours were cut. Plus, my father had a heart attack. It's been really hard."

"I spoke with the school and your position has been deemed one that is to be cut from the budget."

"I do a lot here, though. Who would do my job without my position existing?"

"They'll have to figure that out. We just don't have the enrollment we once had in our schools throughout Queens. It's become difficult to sustain things given the bleakness of the situation. Tuition costs have risen, and our student body has lessened quite a bit. We're fighting to stay afloat."

"I see. So how much time do I have?"

"We would need you to finish up today and then, I'm asking you to resign from the position. You would have to write a letter stating that you are leaving the position."

"Resign?"

"It's not something I would normally ask but when I originally got you the job, I assumed it would be temporary until you found something else. You've been here for years now and we've accommodated you financially by maintaining your employment."

"Would I get unemployment?"

"If you resign, you would not. We don't want to go the route of unemployment. We would rather just resolve this between us. I'm happy to hear you are living with your parents. This means that you will have a place to live. We were worried about that for a few months."

"You've been planning to let me go for months?"

"It's nothing personal. It's simply a budget thing."

"So, I'm expected to resign without as much as this week's pay."

"We can pay you for the week if you need the money. That's not a problem."

"That would really help. I do have bills other than the rent I used to pay."

"I'll go get $200 from petty cash and the principal will sign off on it."

Father Matthew went inside the principal's office and, within five minutes, came out with an envelope with two one hundred dollar bills inside of it.

"Good luck, young man," Father Matthew said to Peter as he handed him the envelope.

Father Matthew asked for the letter of resignation to be filled out in the school office. Peter, not knowing what else to do, agreed to write the letter.

Peter was really frustrated now. He had just met a girl he liked and now he was losing his job. He was trying, within himself, to find a way to tell his parents, but he was so disappointed for not seeing things clearer. He felt that he should have noticed that they most likely cut his hours for a reason. He should have saw this coming.

Feeling nervous, Peter was leaving the school feeling saddened. He wanted to make a good impression on Alicia, and he did, but now he would have to tell her he was let go from his job without even the ability to get unemployment compensation.

Peter went on to his phone and scrolled through his contact list where he found Teresa's number. He decided to text her before getting on the train to go home. He didn't feel ready to go home at that particular moment in time.

Hi Teresa. Are you still working? I'd like to see you. I know it's been a long time.

Within five minutes, Teresa asked for his name. When he said his name was Peter, she didn't recognize who it was. She wrote back.

I don't remember you. I'm at a new address now. Still in Queens. I'm in Kew Gardens. Are you interested in seeing me? If so, I'll give you the address.

Peter confirmed an appointment with Teresa at her apartment via text message. Their scheduled meeting was due to arrive in one hour's time. He didn't have any cash on hand other than the $200 in the envelope which he planned on giving Teresa for an hour of her time. He was extremely sad and stressed. He needed to try to confide in her. He wasn't ready to go home to his parents yet.

When Teresa opened the door of her apartment, she realized that she recognized Peter.

"I remember you. You're the guy who took me to the diner a few years ago."

"Yeah. It's me, Peter. I'm surprised you didn't remember my name."

"Tom, Dick, Harry, Peter. I can't keep all the names straight. I do remember you by face," she said to him.

"It's $200, sweetie."

"I know. I wanted to know if we could talk instead of having sex," he said as she started to open the robe she was wearing.

"It's your dime. I don't have much to talk about these days."

"Do you remember you texted me a few years ago?"

"I texted a lot of guys. I can't keep them all straight like I said."

"Well, you texted me. I always thought about answering your text back then, but I was afraid to."

"Just give me the money, honey."

Peter handed her the $200. She took it and closed her robe up. She took the money over to a dresser drawer which she opened. She put the cash in a roll of bills with the other money she had accumulated. Peter sat on a chair in the middle of the room.

"How have you been?"

"Peter. Don't try to be cute. Why don't we just fuck? It's so much easier for both of us."

"You had texted me something a few years ago. Something about needing help. Do you remember?"

"I don't remember last week, let alone several years ago."

"OK. That's fair to say. So, I guess there's no hard feelings then."

"Hard feelings about what?"

"Not answering your text message."

"How could there be hard feelings. It's always been business between us."

"I know. Anyhow. That's my last $200. I lost my job today."

"I'm sorry to hear that."

"Yeah. I have to get home to see my parents and tell them the bad news. They're going to be so disappointed in me."

"Not as disappointed as my parents probably were in me. Believe me, I wouldn't beat yourself up too much. There are other jobs out there I'm sure."

"I know. It just feels so disheartening that at my age, I'm just getting beat up every day by life. One punch at a time."

"If it's any consolation, the money's going to help me feed my daughter so you're doing a good thing today."

"You have a daughter?"

"Yes. Her name is Samantha."

"Do you have a picture of her?"

"I don't mix business with pleasure. I would never show a client my daughter's face."

"Really? Why not?"

"The creeps I've met lately are the last people I would want to know anything about my daughter. I love her name, but I shouldn't have shared it with you. I run my trap too much."

"Do you want to talk about it?"

"You're funny. You're going to pay me to be my shrink. That's different."

"I wasn't going to get too deep into it. I just thought I could help."

"I can still give you a blowjob if you want."

"No. I'm just feeling lost. Maybe coming here was a mistake."

"Like I said, whatever you do, my daughter gets another week of food thanks to this visit so don't feel like you did a bad thing."

"Do you still have that pimp you used to have back then?"

"I don't want to talk about my business. If you must know, he died, though."

"I won't ask how. Why don't you consider breaking out of the business? If for nothing else, do it for your daughter."

"Let's talk about you. You're the one who came to see me because you needed something. How can I help you?"

"Let me take you on a date again sometime."

"How is that going to work? I thought you had no money."

"I forgot about that."

"No money means we won't be dating anytime soon, honey."

"I just wanted to clear that up. I thought maybe when you texted me that there was a reason you did. I always wanted to know that reason."

"You have the same color eyes as my daughter."

"I do?"

"Yeah. They're really beautiful."

"Should I get going?"

"You have a few minutes left. Don't run away quite yet."

"I thought you'd want me to go. You have my money."

"I do have your money. I always thought you were a nice guy. It's a shame life isn't working out for you. I wish it was."

"Thanks. I'll get something soon. I just don't want to be too much of a burden on my parents. I moved back in with them."

"You should be happy they took you in."

"I'm extremely grateful."

"You should be."

"Well, it was great seeing you. I think you helped me. I just wanted to talk to someone. This whole thing of not having medical insurance is going to kill my parents emotionally. That will make them madder than anything else. I have to let them know as soon as I can."

"You get home to them, then. It was nice seeing you. Good luck, Peter."

"Good luck to you, too," he responded as they walked over to the door and she proceeded to let him out of the apartment.

When Peter left, Teresa started thinking about the physical similarities her daughter had with Peter. From the structure of their faces to the shape of their eyes, they seemed to have striking resemblances to one another. She had never known the identity of her daughter Samantha's father. She wondered if it was Peter. She started to cry as her cell phone rang.

She stored Peter's number in her cell phone again since she had deleted it several years back. She wondered if he would call her with better news over the next few months. She wanted him to be successful, and she hoped he would call her back one day.

Chapter 40

When Peter arrived home that evening, Megan wondered why he seemed distraught. His face looked sad, and he appeared to be exhausted to her.

"Did they work you hard today, dear?"

"No. It's a lot worse than that, Mom."

"What happened?"

"They let me go."

"Oh, no. Don't worry. There are a few places here on the Island that are hiring. That Long Island Railroad was eating into your money too much anyway."

"Thanks for taking it so well."

"You'll just get unemployment to carry you over until you find something. Did they say when the medical will run out?"

"I will get a job. Don't worry about unemployment. I think my medical is paid for another 30 days. Don't worry."

"You're entitled to unemployment."

"OK. If nothing pans out in a week, I'll put in an application for it," Peter said even though he knew it was a lie.

"Your dad will be home soon. I guess I'll let him know."

"Could you tell him tomorrow? I just want peace for tonight until I have to deal with reality."

"I could wait but if I do, you just tell him tomorrow yourself, OK?"

"Will do, Mom."

When he went to his bedroom, Peter received a text message from Alicia asking him how he was doing. Peter didn't respond to it right away. He was just going to spend the rest of the evening relaxing and thinking about ways he could improve his life. He was going to try to figure out what he wanted to do next versus what he actually could do next from a realistic standpoint.

Both of Peter's parents suggested that he make an attempt to go out on another date with Alicia. Peter's parents believed that it would help make him feel better and that she might even have suggestions on what he could do next for work. He didn't tell Alicia on the phone that he lost his job. Instead, he set up a date like everything was normal for that upcoming Sunday afternoon.

Peter met Alicia at a local bowling alley that Sunday. Peter paid for two games upfront as well as the bowling shoes they needed. He put the expenses on a credit card. While they were bowling, Alicia asked him how work was going.

"I have some bad news, Alicia. I got let go."

"You got let go?"

"Yep."

"Why didn't you tell me?"

"It doesn't matter. I'll find something new. Something great. Soon."

"It's not so easy to find a job. How long do you get unemployment for?"

"It's OK. I'll find something soon."

"Let me give you some money for today," Alicia said as she took a 20 dollar bill out of her purse.

"Not necessary. I asked you out and it's my responsibility to pay."

"Why did you ask me out? You could have just invited me over your house for dinner or something."

"I don't know if having dinner with my parents would be a good idea right now. They're worried about me."

"I'm worried about you, too."

"Don't be. Please. It's all good," Peter said as he bowled a strike that current frame.

When their two games ended, Peter and Alicia were walking in the parking lot. They walked over to the car Peter took Alicia on the date in.

"I heard Wendy's is hiring for an Assistant Manager."

"Thanks. I'll look into it," Peter said feeling guilty for not telling her that he lost his job sooner.

"Well, I guess we'll eat home tonight then," Alicia said as Peter started the car.

"That sounds good. Thanks for coming out today," Peter told her.

When they were driving back, there was a lot of silence in the car. Alicia didn't have much to say on the ride back. She was feeling a little let down by the fact that Peter had lost his job. When Peter dropped her home, she told him that she'd call him, but days passed, and Peter didn't get so much as a text message from her.

Peter seriously considered working for Wendy's although he didn't have fast food experience. He was hoping that if he got hired there, he would get trained for the job as he didn't have any real management experience either. His age could have seemed to make him ideal for a management position, but his past work history said the opposite.

Chapter 41

Andrea and God were speaking about Peter's disappointing descent into depression.

"He's getting closer to the age where he will have to marry," Andrea said.

"What am I going to do? Let him die again?"

"You could just leave him be. If nobody kills him this time, maybe he'll get a chance at a normal existence one day. Peter's the definition of a late bloomer."

"It wasn't my intention to have someone kill him the first time. We can't go back on our word, however. We gave him time. John is still within him in one form or another. We've given so much to this man to be grateful for, but he can't see that he has so much love to give. He needs direction."

"Inspire him. Start trying to get through to him in his dreams again. That worked sometimes, back not too long ago as a matter of fact."

"He has all the qualities necessary to be happy, but something prevents him from finding happiness every time. In both lives he's lived."

"Speak to him when he prays in his sleep. I know he often dreams of things far more beautiful than what he's ever had in reality. Try to get through to him. If we can't get through to him, he's coming back and he's going to be more upset than before."

"A life review with him now may make him more understanding on why he's to move on to the next phase of the afterlife."

"True. He would understand that he failed to achieve what was definitely achievable if he had just tried a little harder."

"I want more for him. Some of his qualities remind me of the best people on Earth."

"While other qualities make us cringe more times than not," Andrea stated.

"It's life. It's what we offer our children, and it can be overwhelming, sometimes, more often than not, as a matter of fact."

"I think this girl, this Teresa, has potential to love him."

"I think she feels something for him, and I know he feels something for her."

"Let's try to get this show on the road for them. I'm getting antsy and I don't want Peter's parents to have to attend their son's funeral."

"Agreed. Let's do this the best way we can. For Peter's sake."

"For Pete's sake, did you have to say that?"

"Very funny. On to the next case, now."

Chapter 42

Peter finally, after two months, found himself on a job interview at a shipping company which sold things on eBay. This job was located in Manhattan. Recently, Peter had been having dreams of coming back to work in Manhattan again and now, with this interview, that was a possibility.

After a successful interview with the company, Peter got hired and was even promised a benefits package after 90 days of successful employment. It all seemed too good to be true, but it was really happening.

Peter had lost touch with Alicia. Although she called him once after their date at the bowling alley, he decided not to return the call. As a result, she moved on and started dating new people. Eventually, Alicia found someone. Peter discovered this on her Facebook page a month after he got the new job.

In between his time working, Peter became obsessed with trying to find out his true purpose in life. He didn't feel anybody understood what he was going through in life although his parents told him they did. At times, his dreams seemed more real than what was going on in actuality. Peter wanted to make some aspects of his life better than they had been. He was determined in finding out how to do this.

Since he had run up a tab with his parents during the months he was unemployed, Peter didn't have a lot of disposable income. After having a dream of Teresa one night, he felt determined to go to Queens and see her again. With or without money, he was determined to try to see her.

One seemingly uneventful Tuesday night, Peter made his way over to Teresa's apartment in Queens. He was hoping she still lived there as he walked into the building as someone was coming out. He made his way up to her apartment. He listened against her door to see if he could hear any voices from inside the apartment, but he didn't. He sat outside her door for a few minutes. As he was sitting on the floor outside her apartment, he saw someone come out from the apartment next to hers. He didn't want to make a scene in front of the neighbor, so he knocked on Teresa's door pretending he had just gotten there. Teresa opened the door wearing a set of headphones. She had been listening to music. She turned down the sound of the music.

"What are you doing here?"

"I've been thinking about you a lot, recently, Peter said."

"You're going to be bad for business," she said as she asked him to go into her apartment.

"Why are you here? You want to see me? You call and make an appointment first, like everyone else," she continued.

"I missed you so much, Teresa."

"Great. After a lot of time passes, you seem to miss me but what about the call you should have returned. The call those years back."

"What call are you talking about?"

"C'mon. You know which call I'm talking about."

"OK. I thought I was going to have a normal life that day. I chose to ignore your call so I could try my hand at some sort of normalcy with another girl. Guess what? I don't want normal anymore. That's what I've learned."

"You don't want normal now. What do you want from me? Do you even have any money?"

"Is that all that matters to you. Because, yes, I have money."

"You have money? You mean, you found a job."

"So, you remember me enough to know I was looking for a job."

"Of course, I remember you. Look, I play dumb sometimes, but I don't forget my customers especially when they're as, what's the word, interesting as you are."

"Yes. I got a new job. Why don't we start over? Why don't you just let me take you out again and let's see what happens? I'd really like that."

"There's one question I have for you, though, Peter."

"What is it?"

"Do you think you could introduce me to your parents and how, exactly, would you introduce me to them?"

"If we went out then you'd be my girlfriend."

"And my daughter? How would you introduce her?"

"I don't know how I'd mention it but they're very understanding parents. They'll accept her. In fact, they probably know that dating a girl who's close to my age will most likely involve her having children. You know? They're not unrealistic."

"Two things, then. I want you to meet my daughter. The three of us would go out and see how it goes. My daughter is a good judge of character. I want to see what she thinks of you."

"Great. No problem. What else?"

"I need a job too. I just got strangled by some john this morning. I almost had to call the cops to get him to stop. This job is so done for me. It's time to get out of Dodge."

"Jesus. Really?"

"Yeah. You're here just in time. It's almost like a miracle, in fact."

"I don't know if I could move you in with me right away."

"Listen, meet my daughter first. Then, we can talk. Do you work Saturday?"

"No."

"We'll go to a diner Saturday and see what happens. If things go well, we'll figure something out. I was thinking of moving in with my sister temporarily anyway. She offered."

"We have to get you out of here."

"I'll get out. Let's just see how Samantha likes you first. OK?"

"I'm so happy I came to see you."

"I'm happy to see you too," Teresa said as she gave him a tight hug.

Peter and Teresa sat next to each other on her couch as they were holding hands.

"Do you think this john may come back?"

"I doubt it. I don't think he was in love with me or anything like that, but he wanted it rougher than I'm accustomed to. I'm just glad he's gone. I don't think he'll come back but if he does, I'll scream louder than I've screamed before if I have to."

"Good. We have to get you away from these creeps and weirdos."

"You have a kind heart. I've always noticed that about you."

"Thanks. I try. It's in my nature I guess," he said as he gently kissed her on the lips.

"Can you spot me some money? Just a few bucks, maybe?"

"How romantic? I have about eighty dollars cash. Can that hold you over?"

"Of course. It can. That jerk did actually pay me. I have to give my sister the money for Samantha tomorrow. She needs food and stuff."

"So, your daughter lives with your sister, then?"

"Yes. She couldn't live here, you know?"

"I know," he said as he kissed her on the cheek wondering what he was going to do next in terms of telling his parents about Teresa.

Chapter 43

Peter was happy he was going to go out with Teresa and her daughter Samantha to a local diner that coming Saturday. He decided not to tell his parents he was going on a date. Instead, he told them he was going out with a friend from work. He didn't want to set up expectations that could be weathered by reality. When Peter met Teresa and Samantha outside a diner in Kew Gardens, he was quite happy. He smiled as Samantha reached out her hand to greet him. When they got inside the diner, they were seated at a nice booth by the window.

"It's nice to meet you Peter," Samantha said.

"It's great to see you. You look much bigger than I thought you'd be."

"Mommy always says I'm big for my age."

"So how old are you?"

Samantha started to count on her fingers and showed Peter four fingers.

"So, you're four years old. Wow, that's a great age. I remember when I was four years old," he said.

"How old are you?"

"I'm up there. 30-something. Let's leave it at that."

"Samantha. Don't ask adults how old they are," Teresa said.

"It's an honest question," Peter said.

"I know but it's probably better not to ask adults their age," Teresa stated.

"So, are you in school yet, Samantha?" Peter asked.

"Mommy said I have to go next year."

"That's great. Kindergarten?"

"Yes," Teresa said.

"What's kinder garden?" Samantha asked.

"It's a garden where kids learn their numbers and ABC's," Peter said.

"He's joking. It's not really a garden," Teresa stated.

After they ordered their food, Samantha seemed to enjoy Peter's presence as they waited for their order to arrive. Teresa stopped being nervous and just let them talk to each other about simple things such as what TV shows Samantha watched.

"Do you love my mommy?" Samantha then asked Peter.

"I think I do, as a matter of fact."

"Love takes time, dear," Teresa said.

"Mommy's right but I do have feelings for your mother," Peter told Samantha.

"What kind of feelings?" Samantha asked.

"Yeah, what kind of feelings? Teresa jokingly asked Peter.

"Your mommy is amazing. She makes my heart light up and gives me a warm, gooey feeling inside," Peter said.

"That's funny," Samantha stated.

Peter shared his French fries with Teresa and Samantha when he realized the portion of fries was way too generous. Samantha tried to pour the ketchup from a bottle onto the fries and Teresa helped her get the ketchup out.

When time came for dessert, they each got ice cream scoops. They all got vanilla scoops and loved the scrumptious taste of the ice cream. Samantha was smiling and was happy as she colored a picture in her coloring book while they waited for the check to arrive.

"Can I walk you two home? Peter asked.

"We're going back to my sister's. We have to get on the train two stops," Teresa replied.

"I can take the train with you," Peter said.

"OK," Teresa responded.

When their stop quickly came, Peter asked Teresa if she was alright to get to her sister's house from the train station with Samantha. Teresa confirmed that they'd be fine and told Peter that she'd call him. Peter went back to Long Island feeling happy and was hoping he'd see them again soon.

Chapter 44

After Teresa dropped Samantha back off with her sister, she felt pleasantly surprised that she had a good time with Peter. However, her phone had some text messages on it from clients who were feeling disgruntled she wasn't returning their calls. Teresa thought of throwing her phone away and getting a new one but instead responded to her clients that she wasn't working again until tomorrow. She didn't want to "work" anymore. She needed to come up with a plan to get out of her business once and for all. It was time to embrace some sort of normal life. She had to do it for her daughter, if not for herself as well.

Back on Long Island, Peter was sitting down in the living room with his parents. His mother was going to be getting ready for work soon while his father was taking a short nap and planned on watching a movie with Peter later that night.

"Mom. I met someone."

"You met someone? That's great. Where did you meet her?"

"I met her online."

"Well, that's how people meet these days. Nothing wrong with that."

"She has a daughter."

"Oh, I see. Well, how do you feel about her?"

"I like the daughter. I really am falling hard for the mother."

"So fast? Don't fall in love too fast. It's never a good thing. Take things slow."

"I know. The only thing is I'm going to be 40 in a few years, and I don't want to take things so slow that I end up 40 and alone, you know?"

"I hear you. I have to work tonight but, until tomorrow, just think things through. Me and your father will support you in your decision but just make sure it's the right decision, OK?"

"OK, Mom."

Peter hated that he lied to his mother about where he met Teresa. He felt that he had to lie. He believed there was no way that his parents would accept the truth. Teresa was the only girl he truly felt he understood. He realized she had lived a hard life. Peter wanted to be there for her and Samantha if them being a family was any real possibility.

Teresa texted Peter later on that evening. She wrote him a message.

Do you think we could all go out again next weekend? I think Samantha would like that. Maybe we could all go to a movie. My sister would like to meet you too. Do you think you would be interested in that?

Peter replied back to her. He told Teresa that he'd love to see her and Samantha again. Peter didn't want to get into Teresa's personal business. He didn't ask what she was doing about her "job" although he wondered how she could slip out of it altogether and start a new life. Peter went online and looked at the adult website where he had originally found her. He was glad he didn't see an ad from her on there anymore. Perhaps, they really could be a family if there was a suitable way out of the business for Teresa.

Peter texted Teresa.

I wanted to talk to you about a few things. Do you think we could meet up sometime this week? I just wanted to see how you feel about some things that were on my mind.

Teresa invited Peter over to her place Monday night to discuss what was on his mind. She knew he would probably be bringing up some difficult questions, but she knew she needed to answer them for him. However, she wasn't sure answering them right now was a good idea.

When Peter showed up to see her, she let him in. He looked extremely nervous to her as he sat down on the couch in her living room.

"I don't know where to begin," Peter said.

"Why don't we not talk about what's on our minds? I know that if we do talk about all the obstacles to being together that we will never be together."

"You're right. I guess I'm just wondering if it's all even possible."

"We can live together on our own one day. Just let's see if we want to live together on our own one day. You know what I mean?"

"I do. Let's see what happens, I guess. One day at a time. I'm just worried about my parents and what they think."

"You have to cut the cord one day and now is as good a time as ever."

"I know. I just thought I cut the cord a while back and now that I'm living with them again and, possibly, leaving them again, I want to make sure I do it right this time."

"Are your parents the only thing holding you back from wanting to know me better?"

"I guess I wanted to know if you had a record?"

"A record?"

"A police record for what you've been doing for work."

"Why would you want to know that? Does it really matter?"

"I guess not."

"I did some time but not a lot. I know it may affect me getting another job right away, but I'm determined to make it work."

"I want to make it work so much."

"So do I."

"What else is on your mind?"

"I had a dream the other night," Peter said.

"What about?"

"We once had a conversation about living past lives and the more I think about things and the more I dream about things I've never experienced, the more I believe I've led another life."

"What are you dreaming?" Teresa asked as she sat beside him on the couch.

"I have visions of a train station sometimes and there's a lot of commotion. I don't know where, exactly, I fit into the dream, but I see a subway station with a lot of chaos and people running. I've never mentioned it, or even admitted it to myself, but I see these things in my dreams quite frequently."

"I don't know how to interpret dreams. I definitely believe in past lives and that people are not, only living life once. There's more to life than meets the eye."

"How can you be so sure?"

"I just feel it."

"I don't know. I know one thing, though. I really like your daughter. She's a good kid."

"Thank you. Do you ever dream that you had kids in your past life?"

"No. I never do. Though, I always wanted to have a child and knowing you and Samantha now gives me the chance to be there for a child. That's something that I've always felt was important in my life. At one point, I knew I'd probably never have children of my own. But now, I'm excited at the possibility of being there for Samantha."

"I'm so happy to hear you say that. It's what I always wanted for her."

"It's what every parent wants for their child. To have someone to be there for a kid. I mean it's so important. Do you know what I mean?"

"Yeah, I do."

"Let's just forget I was worried and enjoy tonight together. Do you want to cuddle?"

"I'd love that," Teresa said as Peter put his arm around her, and they sat together on the couch for about two minutes before starting to kiss each other.

Chapter 45

Peter left Teresa's apartment to go back to Long Island after they had made love. He felt a powerful connection with Teresa that he was determined to turn into something good in his life. Although his parents would have their own opinion of her when they met her, Peter was more concerned that the connection he had with Teresa would be a lasting one as his parents were starting to get a little older in age with his father recently having had physical health problems.

When Peter dreamt next, he was seeing the subway station again amidst a lot of screaming people in the background. Images of Teresa started flickering through his mind and then, he even briefly thought of Meredith before waking up. He had no idea why Meredith was coming into his dreams since he had hardly known her. He felt something was happening in his current life that had some connection to a possible past life. He wasn't sure. He just knew that sometimes he dreamt about people and experiences he had little recollection of. It all seemed to have some relevance even though he wasn't sure what the meaning of everything he envisioned was in his current life.

While Peter was working, Teresa was in her apartment trying to no longer work. She consistently got telephone calls and text messages from her old clients. She wanted nothing more than to disconnect her number. She didn't want to talk to these men. She wanted to move forward and try a new job out for herself. She had no idea what she wanted to do but she wanted to do something in customer service, perhaps, as she felt she had strong skills interacting with people.

Teresa decided to go over to her sister's apartment to see her daughter. When she was exiting her building, she saw one of her old johns, a 55-year-old heavy set man named Ralph, waiting in front of a parked car. She walked fast and then Ralph started following her.

"Why aren't you answering my calls?"

"Look, I'm sorry, Ralph. I'm not interested in meeting anymore. I'm starting my life over. It has nothing to do with you," she said as she continued walking away from him as he was following her.

"You don't get to say when you stop working."

"Excuse me," Teresa said as she turned around and faced Ralph.

"I've been seeing you for five years now. I've lent you thousands and given you more than that to feed and clothe your daughter."

"I traded services for that money," she said quietly to him.

"No. I've sacrificed a lot for you."

"I paid you back every penny with my service."

"I think you owe it to me to take my money and go upstairs with me," Ralph said.

"I want out."

"You don't get out so easily after all I've done for you."

"I understand what you mean. Things change, though. I have a boyfriend, now."

"A boyfriend?"

"Yes."

"Girls like you don't have boyfriends."

"What do you mean? Girls like me?"

"You're a whore. That's what you do. You could never be with just one man," Ralph stated.

Teresa started crying and Ralph took her hand. He placed two 100 dollar bills in her hand, and said, "Now, let's go upstairs for an hour then you can go wherever you want to go."

Teresa wiped away tears and started to think of her daughter. She wasn't thinking of the emotional aspects of her daughter's needs but rather the financial ones as she took his hand and walked back to her apartment with Ralph.

In the apartment, Ralph had taken off his clothes as Teresa sat on the bed. She looked over to the bowl of condoms on her dresser and took one out. She unwrapped it and placed it on Ralph's erect penis.

"Are you feeling better now, baby?" Ralph asked.

"Yeah. I guess so," she said as she started to perform oral sex on him.

Teresa had lost all of her drive to give up working and knew that money wouldn't come to her as easily as this in another profession. She knew Peter had a job, but she also knew it probably wouldn't cover the expenses she wanted to take on such as a private school for her daughter, Samantha. She needed to think things through a little more.

Chapter 46

When Peter texted Teresa after work, she took over twenty minutes to respond. Peter didn't think much of it and was happy to set up a date with Teresa for that coming Saturday. Teresa was going to bring Samantha. They were going to see a movie in Queens at the Long Island City theater.

Peter waited in front of the theater where he was going to meet Teresa and Samantha. They were about three minutes late when he saw them coming up the block to meet him.

"Hi, guys. Thanks for coming out."

"Hi, Peter," Samantha said as Teresa kissed Peter on the cheek to greet him.

They went inside and Peter asked them if they wanted popcorn. Samantha said she wanted a kid's combo while Teresa asked him to get her a Coke.

After they obtained their concession items, they walked over to the theater showing a new animated movie Samantha had been yearning to see. They sat down in their seats and Teresa felt secure in the moment feeling that what happened with Ralph was over. She could still move on with Peter if she tried hard to do the right thing.

During the movie as Samantha was eating popcorn, Peter looked at Teresa and believed there was a moment between them happening as she looked deep into his eyes. Peter leaned in and kissed her. Samantha continued watching the movie and she didn't realize what her mother and Peter were doing.

Peter held Teresa's hand after they kissed and tried to see what was happening in the animated film that was playing on the screen. Peter asked Samantha who the bunny was that was on the screen.

"That's Peter Rabbit. You, of all people, should know, Peter" Samantha said.

They all laughed as the movie soon came to its conclusion. As they exited the theater, Peter asked if he could take them back on the train to Teresa's sister's house.

"No, it's OK. Why don't you let us go and call me later on tonight?" Teresa replied.

"Call you tonight?"

"We need to talk about a few things, Peter. Nothing bad. Don't worry."

"I'm not worried. I had a good time. Did you like the movie, Samantha?"

"It was so cool. Thanks for taking me. See you soon," she said as her mother took her hand and the two of them walked towards the subway station as Peter stood there watching them leave.

Teresa texted Peter a few hours later.

I don't know what to do, Peter. I can't really move in with my sister right now.

Why not? Peter texted her back.

Call me.

Peter called her. She seemed upset as she was seemingly breathing somewhat irregularly in his opinion.

"What's wrong?"

"I don't want to move with my sister. I thought it would be good. I don't want her in my business too much."

"What business don't you want her in?"

"I don't want her budding around in my love life or my personal life. I want to try to get a job."

"Jobs don't happen overnight. How much is your apartment?"

"$1250 a month."

"Geez. I couldn't even afford that for myself."

"I know."

"Well, I could see if you could move in with me."

"That would be nice but I'm not sure your parents would approve of me. Do they know I occasionally smoke?"

"I didn't know you smoke."

"See. We don't know each other well enough, yet and I'm so scared."

"Don't be. We like each other. There's nothing you could tell me about yourself that could change that."

"I'm not so sure, Peter."

"Why don't we see if we could get an apartment together somewhere?"

"I could pay 800 to 900 dollars a month myself."

"Where would I get the difference? That's the big question."

"Why don't you apply for assistance? There's a fund at my old church for people who are on hard times. I could see if they could help us."

"That would be great, Peter. I don't know how much they could help us with but anything to help us until we get on our feet would be really helpful."

"I'll call them tomorrow."

Peter called Joyce, the secretary from the old church he used to attend. She vaguely remembered him as he tried to tell her who he was.

"I attended church there for a while and know Father Matthew really well."

"I'll pull your record. What's your name again?"

He told her his name and she found his file on the computer.

"That file seems to be from some time ago. It's been a while since you've given a donation. Anyway, how can I help you?"

"I was wondering if there was still a fund the church had for people who are on hard times. I read about it in the church bulletin once."

"We have a food pantry but there's no fund anymore. We discontinued that program a little while ago."

"I see."

"Is there anything else you need, Peter?"

"No, thank you, Joyce," he said as he hung up the phone.

Peter didn't really have a clue how to help Teresa and knew calling the church was probably not going to work out. He didn't know how to ask his parents for money when they, themselves, were struggling. He started to think that maybe it was a bad idea to get involved with Teresa.

Chapter 47

Teresa was sitting in her apartment scrolling through her phone and looking for clients to delete from her "contacts." She quickly eliminated most of them from her phone but held on to a few in case she was desperate for money. She realized she would most likely have to live in an apartment with Peter. Although he couldn't afford much for rent, she believed she could try to get "on her feet" and then, possibly within a year or two, they could move to a better place.

When Peter texted her to let her know the church idea wasn't going to work out, she called him.

"Hello," he answered.

"Peter, I think we could make this work. Let's just get a place, any place."

"Really?"

"Yeah, we can do anything we want to if we're together, you know?"

"What do you mean?"

"We can have a good life together and then, one day, Samantha could live with us. It could all work out, you know?"

"I hope so. I had doubts when I got the bad news from the church."

"Don't have doubts. Let's start thinking positive for a change."

"Sounds like a plan," Peter said.

When Peter told his parents about the probable move to Queens with Teresa, they were more receptive to the idea than Peter originally had anticipated. They wanted to know more about Teresa, but Peter basically kept things as vague as possible for simplicity's sake. Peter told his parents about Samantha and that Teresa was looking for a job but that's all.

"Why do you like this girl so much?" Josh, Peter's dad, asked.

"I just feel we can communicate to each other and we have this spark. It's something I never felt before with another person," Peter said.

"We understand. You've grown. You're ready to fly with this young woman and we respect that," Peter's mom, Megan, stated.

Peter found an apartment in his price range quickly. His parents helped drive his stuff to the new apartment which Peter signed a one-year lease for. On the day they were to move in, Teresa's sister drove a lot of Teresa's stuff over to the new place as well. Peter was happy to finally meet her sister.

"I'm Peter. It's a pleasure to meet you. What can I call you?"

"I'm Samantha's Auntie Em. Call me Auntie Em."

"Just like in The Wizard of Oz movie? That's great."

"Maybe just, Em, then?"

They both laughed as Samantha was introducing herself to Peter's parents who were filling the dresser with Peter's clothes.

"You don't have to unpack my stuff, guys," Peter said.

"We want to," Megan said.

"I really like your parents," Teresa told Peter as she walked over to them. Teresa had spoken to his parents for a few minutes while Peter was talking to Em.

"I'm just glad the apartment was mostly furnished. We didn't have to move any furniture or buy a T.V. It's a great thing," Peter said.

When Peter was alone for a moment, Em came over to him.

"You're different. I really like you, Peter," she said.

"I hope so. Your sister is a great person."

"She really is. It's about time somebody noticed. Just do your best to try to help her out."

"I will."

"I want to get home, Auntie Em," Samantha said.

"Why, baby?" Teresa asked.

"I'm sleepy. It's been a long day."

"Are you tired because you met my family, Samantha?"

"Silly, Peter. I'm a kid. I don't get tired. I just want to watch Disney Plus."

"Oh, that makes sense, then," Peter said.

Auntie Em and Samantha said "goodbye" to everyone and left the apartment as Josh invited Teresa and Peter to join him and Megan for dinner at a local Italian restaurant.

The four of them walked over to the restaurant which was three blocks from the new apartment. Peter held the entrance door for them as they walked in.

"What do you want to try to do, Teresa?" Megan asked after they all placed their order with the waiter.

"I was really thinking of having another kid, one day."

"Well, not right away, Mom," Peter said.

"I'm not getting any younger, Peter," Teresa said.

"I understand, baby," Peter said.

"Kids are a lot of work but I'm sure you two are up to the task," Josh said after he ordered a bottle of wine to celebrate his son's new beginning with Teresa.

"I know things are going to be great," Megan told them.

"They will be. It'll take a lot of work and perseverance but these two will make it happen," Josh added before he proposed a toast.

"I'd like to propose a toast to my son and my new daughter, Teresa. The daughter I never had but always wanted. I'm looking forward to having you in my family and I can't wait for the day you two make it official with a wedding, if that's what you want. I know you guys are testing the waters right now, but I see passion in your eyes. Both of you have what it takes to make this relationship work. To Peter and Teresa," Josh said as he raised his glass.

Teresa smiled. Peter got a little nervous as he was surprised to be really living something close to what he imagined he wanted his life to be. Peter and Teresa were both happy that night and when they were in the new apartment alone, they felt satisfaction being in each other's company.

Chapter 48

One day, Peter came home from work and smelled something different in the apartment as he opened the door. Teresa was in the bathroom trying to flush something down the toilet as he approached her.

"It's just weed, Peter. I'm sorry. I know you hate drugs," Teresa said.

"Why are you smoking weed?"

"It's just a stress reliever. Nothing more. I promise," she replied.

"It smells awful."

"I know, baby. I knew you were coming home but I thought you'd be here a few minutes later. I can spray the Lysol. It will take away the smell."

"No problem. I don't like you doing drugs. How much was this weed anyway?"

"It wasn't that much."

"Where did you get it?"

"I've had this supplier for years."

"Something I never knew about you. Do you do any other drugs?"

"Weed isn't really a drug and no, I don't."

"Marijuana is supposed to be legalized one day I heard," Peter said as he put his arms around Teresa, and they sat beside each other on the couch.

"I didn't want to do it but sometimes, for me, I feel better smoking it."

"Were you feeling down?"

"A little."

"Why?"

"I was thinking that I don't deserve this new life I've been given."

"Why would you say that?"

"I don't know. I feel like God rewarded me by letting me meet you. I've been really lucky lately. Usually, my name and lucky don't go in the same sentence."

"I love you. Let's go see Samantha tomorrow after work. Maybe we could take a cab over to your sister's."

"That wouldn't be too much money?"

"No. I think I'd like to see Samantha too. Sound good?"

"Yes. Really good," she said as she kissed him on the cheek.

Though the bills were higher than they thought they would be, Peter and Teresa were seemingly happy together. Peter put some of the money he owed for bills on credit cards while he waited for Teresa to find a new job. Although she was looking online, she hadn't received any phone calls recently in response to the resume she sent out. Peter spoke to her about her job search.

"Do you think, maybe, the gaps in your employment record may lead to no call backs?"

"I hope not. I extended the dates a little so there's not too much time unaccounted for," Teresa said.

"I'd really like to get a bigger place one day and have Samantha live with us. It seems like that happening though is so far from really happening. I get sad sometimes."

"I know. I wanted to have another kid soon, too. But, without a job, I know it would be hard on you."

"I read today that a job can't ask you about your history and can only ask if you've gotten in trouble with the law after they hired you. Just ask me before you answer any question like that so I can help you."

"I've been reading up on that. I know it will be fine. Just believe."

"I love you. Let's just take it one day at a time," Peter said.

They kissed each other and cuddled on the bed. Peter felt he was older than he wanted to be during this period of his life, but he felt secure that time would make sense of everything.

Teresa would think about trying to call a client or two from time to time for extra money but hadn't done so since moved in with Peter. She hoped that she put that part of her past behind her successfully. She definitely didn't want a client knowing where she and Peter were living.

When the TV felt like it was on too long, Teresa turned it off hoping Peter would save some money on the electric bill if she didn't run it all day. However, the electric bills were always over $100 a month. Peter complained but knew he was just ranting because he was scared that he would lose his job again. However, luckily, his latest evaluation at work secured him a two dollar an hour pay increase which would definitely help him pay some bills. Things were going well for them for now.

Chapter 49

Andrea was watching them from up above and wondering with God if Peter and Teresa would get married for if they did get married, then Peter would be able to live his life out on Earth successfully.

"They're so close to happiness," Andrea said.

"I knew things would work out for Peter."

"They just have to get married."

"Peter will propose soon. He's that type."

"I know he is. But can he afford to propose?"

"I think so. I've seen so many people on Earth make things happen that seemed so far out of their budgets. I'd like to think of them as miracles. People make miracles every day down there."

"With our help."

"Yes. I'd like to think we help a bit."

"So, you're optimistic?"

"I would say, very."

"Let's just see what happens. It's not Peter I worry about. It's more Teresa."

"I wish the girl could have a little good fortune."

"Let's hope somebody gives her an opportunity. It would be good for her."

Teresa became a little disappointed with her new life as her job prospects waned. She wanted to do a lot of things with her life that would lead to Samantha coming to live with her and Peter. However, judging from the lack of phone calls from job applications she filled out, she believed her life seemed to be destined for mediocrity.

While Peter worked, Teresa tried to keep busy watching television or cleaning the apartment, but she wanted more than that. She took opportunities to visit her daughter at her sister's house two or three times a week.

Over the past few days, Teresa had kept her phone on silent mode so she could ignore messages that were coming in from old clients. Her responses had definitely decreased to one or two a day and she was grateful the correspondence was petering out from the people she had met over the years.

Peter had given Teresa some money to buy food for the apartment and for clothes for herself. However, Teresa had barely any funds left for anything else. She knew she needed more money.

One guy named Ken had been sending her text messages almost every day. He was close to her age and was tall with a husky build. He had a bit of an anger streak in him. She noticed this during a session she had with him where he was quite rough with her physically. However, she was interested in contacting him to see if he had a place for a session with her. Teresa needed the money. She didn't want to bother Peter to give her more cash.

When Teresa sent a text message to Ken, she stated she was working again but only doing "outcalls." Ken responded by saying he had his own place and that she could go there for a session later on that very day. It was about a twenty-minute train ride for Teresa to get there but she set up the appointment with him for a time around when Peter usually was coming home from work. She left a note for Peter that she was food shopping and would be home "within the hour."

When the time arrived for her meeting with Ken, Teresa showed up at his door. He lived in a basement apartment walk in. He let Teresa in and had an ugly intensity about him that scared her somewhat. He looked disgruntled as he started to talk to her.

"Where have you been? I've been texting you."

"Sorry. I've been really busy."

"Doing what?"

"Trying to get a regular job."

"I see."

"Get naked for me, baby. Do you have the cash?"

"It's in my top drawer."

"OK, baby. Can you get it for me?"

"Go ahead. Take it from the drawer. It's on the left."

Teresa walked over to the drawer and opened it. There was no visible money in it.

"OK, what's going on? It's not here."

"Why have you been hiding from me? Do you not like me?"

"I like you, baby but I need my money."

"You think it's OK to just ignore me?"

"I said I was sorry. If you don't have the cash, I'll just get out of here."

"Do you still have that pimp you were telling me about?"

"Yes. Dexter's in the car outside waiting for me. I actually have to get out of here. I have another appointment and you're acting weird," she said as she started to make her way to the door.

"I think you're lying."

"Should I scream for help now?"

"Nobody would hear you. They're not home upstairs."

"Help!" she screamed.

Ken slapped her and picked her up off the ground. She tried to scratch him with her fingernails, but he didn't budge. He carried her over to the bed and threw her on it.

"Guess what, bitch? I'm not paying today."

Teresa reached out and grabbed a pen that was on a table next to the bed. He tried to grab it from her, but she clicked it into his neck hard.

Ken screamed, "You bitch!"

Teresa got up and ran over to the kitchen where she grabbed a knife from one of the drawers. She pointed it at Ken. He grew increasingly more intense as he reached out to grab her by the throat. She slashed the knife down his arm and his blood began coming out. He took his hand and put it on his arm to try to stop the bleeding. She ran out of his apartment and down the street. She was worried he was going to follow her, but he wasn't coming out. She ran away straight down the street as fast as she could to escape.

As Teresa was running, she knew she had a bruise that Peter would notice if she went straight home. She also knew that if she went to the police, she might get in trouble even though she did what she did in self-defense. She was scared if she told the cops why she was there to begin with that she may get arrested again.

When Teresa got to a supermarket, she went inside and called her sister to tell her she was coming over to see her. Em didn't mind although she was a little surprised that Teresa was coming by so late in the day.

Chapter 50

She arrived at Em's house and saw Samantha seated at the dinner table through the window with Em's husband, Harry. Teresa looked in a car window to see how bad her bruise was. She had to tell her sister something about how she obtained the bruise. Her phone was vibrating with text messages. She looked down and read one of them which was from Ken and read:

I'm going to kill you, bitch!

Frightened, Teresa turned off her phone and went into the house. Em noticed her bruise immediately.

"Did Peter fuckin' hit you?"

"Em, calm down."

"I'll send Harry over there to kick the shit out of him. Jesus. It's always the people you'd least expect."

"It wasn't Peter. Let's not talk loud around Samantha, OK?"

"Let's talk upstairs," Em said as they walked up the staircase to the main bedroom of the house.

"What the hell is going on, Teresa?" Em asked as she closed the door to the room.

"I went with a client and he hit me."

"A client? I thought you were done with that shit."

"I needed some quick cash."

"Did you ask Peter?"

"No."

"So why did he hit you?"

"There's more. I sliced his arm with a knife."

"Oh my God."

"I also stuck a pen in his neck."

"We're going to have to call the police. You know that."

"We can't call the police. They'll wonder why I was there in the first place."

"OK. So, if he calls the police on you, they'll come after you anyway."

"I don't know if he'll call the cops. We should wait and see."

"We shouldn't wait and see. Then it will look like you did something wrong."

"I did do something wrong."

"You did. But it was nothing that was going to hurt anyone. I assume that Peter doesn't know, right?"

"You assume correctly."

"Stay here for a minute. I will talk to Harry."

"Do we really have to bring Harry into this?"

"Look. You have a daughter who is depending on us. We can't get involved with helping you escape from the police or we'll lose her. I want to be there for Samantha. I don't know what you want to do. I think it's best to call the cops."

"What if we didn't tell Harry?"

"We have to get someone's advice. You could try to talk to Peter and explain you were back selling yourself again when you're supposed to be faithful to him."

"I guess I'll have to take that chance then, Em."

"How bad did you stick him with the pen?"

"It was pretty bad. He sent me text messages. I turned my phone off."

"Put the phone back on. Let's see what he said."

As Em and Teresa were getting ready to look at the text messages from Ken, Harry was watching television downstairs with Samantha. Even though, Harry heard some shouting between Em and Teresa, it was nothing he hadn't heard before.

As they scrolled through the four text messages, Ken wrote Teresa, they both got increasingly nervous. Ken's most dire text message to Teresa read:

I will find you and I will kill you, bitch.

"We have to go to the cops. It was self-defense. They'll understand that, for sure," Em said.

"And, I guess I have to tell Peter. It's over for me."

"There's nothing wrong with telling him the truth. If he loves you, he'd understand."

"He'd understand that I went to go fuck some other guy for money."

"He always knew what you did for a living before you guys moved in together."

"Fine. Let's call the police. Go, tell Harry."

"I am going to call my neighbor, Patricia, and see if she can watch Samantha for a couple hours."

"Why?"

"I'm going to drive you to the precinct. I don't want to make a scene having the cops come here. It's not good for the neighborhood."

"Whatever you want to do," Teresa said.

Em went downstairs and asked Samantha if she'd like to go over and play with Patricia's daughter, Jenny. Samantha screamed out, "yes!" Patricia agreed to watch Samantha for a couple of hours after Teresa called her and asked her for the favor.

"What's going on?" Harry asked.

"I'm bringing Samantha to Patricia's then we all need to get in a car and go somewhere," Em said.

"Where? What did Teresa do now?"

"Let me just bring Samantha over there."

Em walked Samantha a few houses down to Patricia's and came back to her home. Harry was looking quite frustrated and pacing back and forth while Teresa was sitting on the couch with her bruise having gotten significantly more noticeable.

"Teresa got into trouble again."

"What kind of trouble?" Harry asked.

"She stabbed someone with a pen," Em stated.

"And I cut his arm too," Teresa added.

"This is it. I don't want you coming around here anymore," Harry explained.

"Listen, honey, it was self-defense. The guy tried to beat her," Em said.

"I thought this guy, Peter, was normal."

"It wasn't Peter," Teresa stated.

Teresa's phone was vibrating with a text message from Peter asking where she was as well as two more threatening text messages from Ken.

"Let's go to the cops now!" Em demanded.

"I don't understand," said Harry.

"Let's just go now," Em said as the three of them got into a car and headed over to the local police precinct to report what had happened.

Chapter 51

Peter was waiting by his phone for hours before he received a text message from Em that they were at the police precinct and that something had happened to Teresa. Peter was concerned but after sending two text messages asking what had happened to her, he received no response.

It was now a half hour after he received the first message from Em, and Peter was frustrated. Peter started to pray to God silently asking Him to "let Teresa be OK."

At the police precinct, Teresa was being held until they could get ahold of Ken. Teresa showed an officer the text messages and he was very concerned about what Ken and Teresa did to each other.

Another office was calling two local hospitals to see if they could find someone admitted there who had the injuries Teresa described. After no hospitals confirmed such a patient, a police car went to Ken's house to see if they could locate him.

When nobody answered at Ken's apartment, the officer went upstairs and told the landlord that they needed to know if anybody was in his apartment. As the landlord walked down the stairs to the basement inside the house, he heard Ken moaning and became immediately concerned. As soon as the landlord let the police know Ken was in there, the cops came into the basement and knocked on the entrance door to the apartment.

"This is the police. Please open up!"

Ken reached up to the door and turned the knob to open it. When the police saw him, he was covered in bloody towels which Ken had placed on his arm to try to stop the persistent bleeding.

Back at the precinct, Teresa couldn't call anybody because her cell phone had been taken by the police as evidence. She wanted to ask to make a phone call to Peter, but she didn't know what to tell him about what had happened.

Back at Peter's apartment, he finally received a phone call from Em who explained the situation to Peter. Em told him everything from the fact that Teresa had went to meet a client for money to the fact that she was bruised and had stabbed the man as well. Peter was frightened for Teresa most of all. He didn't know what would happen. Peter told Em to take care of Samantha and to let him know as details progressed in the situation.

Peter knew he was involved "way over his head" and called his parents to explain what had happened to Teresa. He had to tell them everything about how he really met her and that she got herself into a pretty bad situation.

"Oh my God," Megan said when he told her about the fact that Teresa was involved in a confrontation with one of her clients from the days when she was a prostitute.

"I'm so sorry," Josh told Peter.

"Why are you sorry? I just can't believe you lied to us," Megan said.

"What was I supposed to tell you?" Peter asked.

"The truth," Josh said.

"How could I have ever told the truth about something like this?"

"You know we raised you to do the right thing in life. Always."

"I know. But the right thing doesn't work for everyone. I tried to do everything right in life and nothing ever happened. It took me meeting a prostitute to find someone I could love. And she went to sleep with another man to make money. I feel like a fool, but I have to see her side."

"Do you really love her now even knowing she went to have sex with someone behind your back?"

"I don't know. She needed money for something. I don't know for what. Maybe for her daughter. I don't know. There must have been a reason."

"She has issues. Serious, serious issues. That's the real reason, Peter. You can't have a relationship with a girl like that."

"I want to see what happens. I want to hear her side. Then, I want to make a decision. A decision of my own," Peter said.

"I don't know what's going to happen here. Let us know when you find out, I suppose," Josh stated.

When Em finally called Peter back the next day while he was working, she told him that the police were keeping Teresa in jail and that she had to see a judge to determine the outcome of her fate. She had been accused of assault on Ken for slashing him with the knife.

Chapter 52

Andrea and God were looking at the situation that Peter found himself involved in. They were concerned for both him and Teresa.

"I knew that Teresa was going to let herself fall prey to her desire for money. What was she going to do with the 200 dollars anyway?"

"I don't know, Andrea. I don't understand why people think that they need money all the time. Sometimes, if they could just let money stay out of the equation for at least a little while, things would be more peaceful. Don't you think?"

"We're looking at America now and wondering what the country needs to do to maintain its sanity. Every day, people are worried about money and hurting each other over money. I'm starting to think it's all so wrong."

"Money is a concept that was created with noble intentions in mind, for sure. People become obsessed. Teresa has a strong heart. Her urges to give to her daughter are so admirable. But what she did to get money all those years, it was such a mistake."

"Samantha, though. That beautiful child that's come from everything. Thank God, you, and fate for Em and Harry. They keep things sane when things are anything but."

"I have to have faith in Peter. He must make the right decision for himself. It's getting late for him to meet someone else but I'm curious to know if he really loves this woman enough to make the ultimate sacrifice and stand by her."

"What do you mean the ultimate sacrifice?"

"Sacrificing the dream that everything will be perfect in a relationship. It's something he will have to do if he is to remain with Teresa."

"Many people accept others as companions for themselves. I guess it has a lot to do with finding someone you can actually live with."

"These two can live with one another. They have that potential. Let's see where this goes. I wish I had more control over where this will ultimately lead. I am doing everything in my power to make it work."

"That's all you can do."

Peter went to see his parents the following Saturday. He hadn't heard from Em and was quite concerned. Megan and Josh were both home and wanted to try to make Peter see a reason to begin anew. Peter took a seat on their living room couch as his mom began to speak to him.

"I think you should move on, Peter," Megan said.

"I thought Dad said Teresa was like a daughter to him. What happened?"

"If you love her, I'll support you, but I don't know if she's what you need to be happy," Josh stated.

"I don't know what's going to make me happy. I know I've tried so hard to live a normal life and have struggled so much."

"Struggle but don't settle, honey," Megan said.

"I love this woman. I love her daughter. I care about them deeply."

"Why haven't you heard what's going on with her, then?"

"I don't know, Mom. Em hasn't called me. I should really call her and see but I don't want to intrude."

"You have to intrude if you love her," Josh said.

"OK. When I go home tomorrow, I'll give Em a call," stated Peter.

"What do you want for dinner tonight, honey?"

"I don't know, Mom. Do you really want to cook? Why don't we just order out?"

"Like pizza or something?"

"Yeah, Dad. That would be perfect."

"Daddy knows what you like to eat, dear. Pizza will be fun," Megan said.

Peter and his family watched television sitcoms that evening before dinner and after they ate their pizza slices, they went back to the couch to see if they could watch a movie together. Peter didn't feel comfortable watching television anymore, though. He was too concerned with Teresa.

"Maybe I should call Em now and see what's going on."

"That's a good idea," said Josh.

Peter called Em's cell phone number. After three rings, she finally answered.

"Hi, Peter."

"How did you know it was me?"

"The caller ID on my cell."

"What's going on with Teresa?"

"She's still in jail, Peter. They set a very expensive bail amount for her. I didn't want to burden you."

"How's Samantha?"

"We didn't tell her everything. Just that mommy went to see an old friend. We haven't got the heart to tell her the truth until we see what the judge says at the sentencing hearing in a couple of weeks."

"Well, what kind of lawyer does she have?"

"She's got a court appointed attorney."

"Is he any good?"

"She seems pretty good. I guess we'll see."

"Why can't they send her home? Is the guy in jail too?"

"Yes, he is."

"I hope he doesn't get out on bail."

"I doubt it. The guy wasn't working full-time I heard. I don't think he has enough money."

"Jesus. All the red tape involved with the courts is going to keep her locked up, isn't it?"

"It was bad enough when it was revealed what she had been doing for a living but then the assault on top of everything. I don't even want to talk about it now, Peter. I'd ask you to see Samantha, but I want to talk to Teresa before we do anything."

"I understand. Thanks for the update. Please call me with any news, no matter what it is."

"I'll do my best, Peter. Thanks for all you did for Teresa."

"I love her."

"We know you do. We know."

"She's in jail," Peter told his parents when he got off the phone.

"You have to stay strong," Josh said.

"Should I try to visit her?"

"Peter, give it some time before you go to see her. She's probably a wreck now," said Megan.

"I'll call Em next week and see what I should do. Teresa must feel so hopeless right now."

"Yes, she probably does, son. You did what you could for her. See what happens but prepare for a worst-case scenario," stated Josh.

"I'll have to look online and see what the worst-case scenario is," Peter said.

"She did a lot of things she shouldn't have done. I'm quite concerned for her," added Megan.

"Can I sleep here tonight? I don't want to go home right now."

"Of course, you can," Josh said.

Chapter 53

Teresa's case was being reviewed for her suggestion that she was acting in self-defense but because of her attack with a weapon, and her history of prostitution, the judge saw her case as a complex one and assigned her an appropriate social worker. They had to determine the state of Teresa's mental health before they could release her from jail.

Peter discovered the news and decided that he wanted to go visit Teresa in jail. He asked Em to tell Teresa to add him to her visitors list so he could go see her.

While visiting Teresa, Em confronted her with the fact that Peter truly loved her and wanted to go see her one day soon.

"I don't want to see him anymore. I'm ashamed of what I have done. I can't believe what I did and how desperate I must have been to go see that loser, Ken."

"Peter won't make any judgments on you. I promise you that. We've already discussed that."

"I know Samantha really likes him. But I don't know if I want to bring him any deeper into my life."

"Why not?"

"There's so more to this story, Em. I think Peter may be Samantha's biological father."

"Why would you say that? I thought you didn't know who the father was."

"Because they look alike, and I never had a client whose condom had fallen off around the time she was conceived except for Peter."

"I don't want to know about whose condom fell off with you. Do you really think he's the father, though?"

"Yes, I do."

"Should I ask him to take a paternity test?"

"It's the only answer. It's the only way I'd know if I want him seeing me or Samantha anymore."

"It's something to consider. It's not the right time to do that. When it is, we'll know. You really should let him come see you. It would mean a lot to him and I think it would make you feel a lot better."

"I'll think about it."

Another week had gone by, and Peter found himself back at his parents' house on the weekend. Peter didn't talk much about how he felt. Rather, he helped his mother go grocery shopping Saturday afternoon and did a jigsaw puzzle with his father on Saturday night while Megan worked.

When Sunday arrived, Peter and his parents attended Sunday mass at the parents' parish on Long Island. Peter thought about a lot of things during the mass and was feeling a little uneasy regarding his relationship with Teresa. When the part of the mass came to shake hands with other parishioners and wish them "peace," Peter felt momentarily puzzled by this part of his religion. He didn't understand the purpose of wishing peace to those around him when he knew that he hardly knew anything about the people whose hands he shook. Maybe it was his own feelings of guilt regarding what sins he had committed but he didn't like wishing "peace" to people he hardly knew. Peter felt the other people in the church had some secrets as well and were possibly just as "sinning" at times as he felt he was himself.

After mass, Megan went home to sleep. Josh dropped her off at the house and then took Peter to a diner for lunch. While they were seated, Peter spoke to his father about what was on his mind.

"I took Teresa and her daughter Samantha to a diner in Queens on a date."

"Oh, that sounds like it must have been nice," Josh said.

"It was."

"So, how are you feeling today?" Josh asked.

"Like I have no answers about what is important in my life anymore."

"Well, have you thought about what you want to do being that Teresa is still in jail?"

"I love her."

"I know you think you love her."

"I do. Nobody else paid attention to me or cared about me until I met her."

"Peter, she was a prostitute. She was paid to pay attention to you."

"Not always. Not every time. She felt something towards me, I know it."

"Why can't you just meet someone who has less of a stressful situation?"

"Because those girls reject me,"

"You're being ridiculous, Peter."

"No. I'm not. I'm being dead serious. Everything revolves around my car, how much money I make or if a girl is attracted to me, physically. Nothing ever seems to concern my personality, my feelings or who I am as a person."

"I understand what you're going through. It took me a few bad dates to finally meet your mother."

"But you did meet her. And you had me before you were my age."

"That's true."

"I'm an outcast. I have nothing going on for myself except my love for Teresa and Samantha. I'm sorry to say but this job of mine is a joke. I go there and make my money and get my benefits, but does it make me happy? No. I give this place five years and they'll probably go out of business."

"Why do you say that?"

"It's been really slow there lately. Sometimes I sit there doing nothing for hours."

"You need to look for things to do there. I'm sure there's something."

After Peter and Josh ordered their food, they began to speak again. Josh was upset with Peter for thinking the way he had been doing so recently.

"You might need some professional help, Peter," Josh said.

"I might. That kind of help won't give me back the years of my life I've lost but it might help me in my future."

"Do you want me to look for a good therapist here on the Island or in the city for you?"

"Not quite yet. I wanted to ask you something, though."

"What do you want to ask me?"

"What did you and Mom think of me these past few years?"

"We love you. You're our son."

"But am I what you expected when you had me?"

"What do you mean?"

"Do I ever make you feel glad that you had me?"

"All the time. We enjoy your company. We love you. We wish things were easier for you but we're always there for you. I hope you know that."

"Why did you have me?"

"We had you because we got married and having a kid was the next logical step I suppose."

"I see."

"What do you mean? I'm sorry. I don't know if that was how I was supposed to answer that particular question."

"Answer it truthfully, of course."

"Well, we wanted someone who would continue our legacy of love. I am happy that you are my son. Don't you ever doubt that, OK?"

"What does Mom think?"

"I can't speak for her but I'm almost certain that she thinks the same thing as me. Don't worry so much. There's our food coming now. Let's get ready to eat."

"Dad. I'm sorry," Peter said as tears fell from his eyes and one rolled down his cheek.

"Why did you say that? You have nothing to be sorry for."

"I'm sorry I wasn't what you wanted."

"Don't say that," Josh said as the waiter put the food on the table.

"I just wish I could have been more."

"You're good enough, Peter."

"I'm not strong enough to live the way that people do. I'm not strong enough to make the money that most people do. I'm not good-looking enough to do what I want to do in life."

"Peter, calm down. Let's eat. I love you. You're fine. Believe me."

"I wish I was fine, Dad."

"I'm sorry. Maybe it was our fault."

"What do you mean?"

"Maybe, we sent you to the wrong schools, put too much pressure on you. I don't know. It may be our fault you're not happy."

"Everything you guys did for me means the world to me. Don't say it's your fault."

"I want you to realize we care about. Do you need a hug?"

"Maybe after we eat," Peter said as he started to smile.

"Why not now?"

"It would be embarrassing. A couple of guys hugging in a diner, you know?"

"We'll hug when we get out of here."

"Thanks, Dad. I love you."

"I love you too, my son," Josh said as he looked at Peter who seemed calm enough now to eat.

Peter felt a little better after he ate and finally hugged his father in the parking lot after their meal. Peter just wanted to know he was loved and he felt his father truly loved him which was the most important thing for him in that moment.

Chapter 54

Em called Peter that night and let him know that Teresa just needed a few more days to decide when a good time for Peter to visit her would be. Peter was thankful and asked her if there was anything that he could do to help her in the meantime.

"We've got everything under control with Samantha. Don't you worry, Peter," Em said.

"Is Teresa going to be OK?"

"I wish we knew that one."

"Well, let me know as soon as you hear anything—good or bad."

"I will, Peter."

"Thank you."

As days passed, Peter hadn't heard anything from Em for a few days until, one day, she called him on a Thursday night.

"I have to tell you something, Peter."

"What is it?"

"I am going behind Teresa's back here, but she said something that may be of interest to you."

"What's that?"

"Samantha. Did she ever tell you about Samantha's dad?"

"No."

"Well, she never knew Samantha's dad. She thought he was a client. In fact, she knows he was."

"Oh, boy."

"That's why I have to ask you a very important and very personal question," Em said.

"Of course, anything."

"Do you ever remember anything about having sex with my sister involving a condom that fell off?"

"Vaguely, but yes."

'What happened if you don't mind me asking?"

"Wow, that is really personal."

"I know but there's a good reason here."

"What's the reason?"

"Would you think a paternity test could be necessary to see if you are Samantha's dad?"

"How could I be Samantha's dad?"

"Well, it only takes one time to create a child as I'm sure you well know, and Teresa can't remember any other client who had a condom that slipped off."

"Was Teresa on any kind of birth control?"

"She didn't have a lot of money as you know. She mostly relied on condoms. Would you be interested in a paternity test?"

"What does Teresa say?"

"She, quite frankly, doesn't want to talk. She thinks you're better off without her. I like you, though. Samantha likes you too. But I like you a lot and am determined to see if there's a reason you would have to be in our lives. Because

Teresa setting you free doesn't sound like the happy ending to this story. Do you know what I mean?"

"I get it. Sure. I'll take a paternity test. What do I have to do?"

"I'll do everything. I'll tell Samantha we're doing a background check on her nationality and I'll swab some DNA from her then I'll personally swab some DNA from you. I'll get it sent off and we just have to wait. It's fairly simple, really."

"What would it prove, though if I was the father?"

"That you have every right to be in her life. If that's something that you want."

"It is. It really is."

"Then, I'll set things up tomorrow after work and come by you on Saturday for my DNA swab."

"What exactly is a DNA swab?"

"It's just a sample of your DNA. I'll rub a swab on your face and get what we need to discover the truth."

"What if I'm not Samantha's dad? What then?"

"Well, then you'd really have to wait until Teresa was ready to see you to talk to her. I think she'd be much more willing if you were the father. I mean, there are some facial similarities between you and Samantha, in case you haven't noticed."

"I noticed the eyes. They seem very much like mine."

"There are other things too. I don't want to get your hopes up. Let's do lunch Saturday afternoon at the diner by your house. We'll see what happens from there. OK? Whatever's meant to be will be."

"Sounds good."

When Peter met Em by the diner Saturday, he asked her if she wanted to take the swabs of DNA from him and then just leave. Em insisted on having lunch with him. As they were seated at a table, they started to talk.

"What's your deal, Peter?"

"What do you mean?"

"Why are you single, involved with my sister of all people? You're not a bad looking guy."

"Thanks for that. I find your sister interesting and I enjoy her company."

"I'm grateful you do. She's going in front of a judge again next week. I'm truly frightened for her. She really hurt that guy, you know?"

"He deserved it."

"He has a lawyer who twisted the story around, but I trust my sister. She wouldn't lie to me."

"How did she ever get involved in what she's gotten involved in?"

"I blame my parents. They didn't challenge her. They raised us both with fantasies of a knight in shining armor coming to save us. My knight never came. Not until I was in my mid 20's. Still not sure he's a knight. However, when Teresa's didn't come at 15, she dropped out of high school. Naturally, my parents got mad but when she ended up living with a 22-year old girlfriend of hers when she was 16, she got involved with people who…well, they were not good for her to get mixed up with if you catch my drift."

"I see. Why didn't your parents try to get her away from this girlfriend?"

"They were just friends. The girl worked somewhere and had promised to get Teresa a job alongside her. But it never happened. She worked for some store which shut down and then the two of them tried selling themselves for extra money.

I don't know why it escalated into what it escalated into, but my parents grew tired of trying to find where she was and to get her to accept that she wasn't a failure. They wanted her to go back to school so desperately."

"She told me had been going back for a GED. How did that work out?"

"It didn't work out so great. She couldn't pass the tests. When you're out of school for long enough, easy tests become that much more difficult."

"I understand."

"Let's order some food, shall we?" Em said when the waitress came over to them.

"About the DNA swab," Peter said.

"Oh, that's why we're here, isn't it?"

"Yes. But, do you think it's a good idea?"

"I do," Em said as she took out a swab to get his DNA sample.

Chapter 55

After Em collected the DNA sample from Peter, they ate and then parted ways. Em asked Peter to come by the lab which was doing the test on Monday before work so he could sign some paperwork for the test to be performed. Em had already gotten Teresa to sign paperwork about obtaining the results when they would be ready. Em had convinced Teresa that it was pivotal for Peter to know where he stood in Teresa's life and to see if he had any biological connection to Samantha.

Peter signed the paperwork Monday morning and the night before he signed it, he prayed to a God that he wasn't sure existed asking Him for the strength to handle the results whatever they may turn out to be.

A social worker named Patricia O'Neill, 37-years old, was working with Teresa and she was given the results of the paternity test to discuss with Teresa. Patricia was walking into the prison to meet with Teresa on a cloudy afternoon. Em was not told the results yet, nor was Peter. Patricia needed to see if Teresa could emotionally handle the result before it would be disclosed.

Teresa was handcuffed when she was brought out to a table by guards so she could sit down across from Patricia. Teresa was very disgruntled and had an unkempt appearance and depressed look on her face.

"Hi, Teresa," Patricia said.

"What's going on?"

"Well, we found out the results of the paternity test."

"And what are they?"

"I need to ask you some questions, Teresa."

"Go ahead."

"Tell me about Peter."

"What is there to tell?"

"Why did you move in with him?"

"He's a nice guy and my daughter seemed to like him."

"Do you like him?"

"I suppose."

"What kind of family would you envision for yourself if the judge was to let you go?"

"I don't know. It's kind of hard to survive if I can't get a job,"

"What if I told you there was a rehabilitation program that could help you get back to work."

"You could get me a job?"

"We could certainly do our best to make you have the requisite skills to obtain gainful, legal work."

"That sounds great."

"I just wonder if Peter is really the best guy for you?"

"Is Peter Samantha's father, or isn't he?"

"That's a good question."

"I'd like to have an answer."

"Are you thinking that if Peter was the father that you would be able to provide a normal life for Samantha?"

"I'd like to hope so."

"I would have to make a recommendation to the judge that you could, in time, be a fit mother for Samantha."

"What do you mean?"

"Your sister, Em, has custody. I was thinking of drawing up a plan upon your release to see if you could gain custody of your daughter in two years' time."

"I would be able to get out of here one day?"

"Of course, you would. It's clear that you acted in self-defense, but we worry about your mental state of health. What led you to prostitution is another concern. It's things like that we worry about."

"It was something I did. It's a part of my past but I've heard from people in jail that it's possible to move on successfully."

"Yes, it is. Who have you been speaking to?"

"I'd rather not say but I have faith that I could overcome my past if I was given a second chance."

"Do you feel more comfortable with your sister, Em, watching Samantha than you do with anyone else right now?"

"Yes."

"OK. We don't know a lot about Peter, but he doesn't have an extraordinary income. That much is certain. He does, however, have paternal rights."

"So he is the father?"

"Yes, he is."

"Maybe we could let him visit Samantha a couple of times until I get out?"

"Therein lies the complexity of the issue."

"What do you mean?"

"Samantha doesn't have a grasp of what her mother is in jail for. Sure, she knows you defended yourself, but she doesn't know much about what you did for a living all your life."

"I don't really want or need her to know that at this point in her life."

"We're in agreeance there, for the most part."

"So, what's the situation? What am I going to do?"

"We're going to let Em in on the news, and, of course, Peter, however, it's not recommended that we tell Samantha, yet. There's a lot of complexity involved in the situation here and we may need to get her some therapy to deal with what's going on."

"Samantha's a strong girl."

'Yes, but she's just a child."

"I understand. When do I get out of jail?"

"We need to see where you would live if you did go home, wherever the best home for you may be. The judge would be depending on my report and an overall evaluation by a psychiatrist. We're thinking of Em possibly taking you in, since you've known her the longest."

"I don't think she would."

"She took Samantha in. She loves you. Don't you realize that?"

"What if I married Peter?"

"Do you think he would marry you?"

"I'm not sure."

"I haven't met Peter, but I would think given the gravity of what happened, he may be a little disappointed in what had happened between you two."

'I love him, and he loves me. What happened with my stupid choices was purely a set of financial decisions that I made. It had nothing to do with hurting his feelings. I never wanted to hurt him."

"I can understand that. I know if you were unmarried and living with your sister, you may be entitled to some benefits until you can stand up on your own two feet again."

"I see."

"I'd like to sit on a session with both you and Peter to discuss the possibilities and reveal the results of the paternity test to Peter."

"Please let Peter know the results immediately. I think meeting with both of us is a good idea at some point, though. I would like to discuss things with Peter. What about my sister?"

"She's in this for sure but I think the two of you, as parents, need to discuss what's best for Samantha with me to see where we stand. You both do have a say as biological parents."

"I'm happy to hear that."

"You are still Samantha's mother. Never forget that."

"I won't."

Chapter 56

Peter was given the news that he was Samantha's biological father by Patricia and Em one late afternoon at Patricia's office in a local hospital. Peter was immensely frustrated but, also, pleasantly surprised. He wished he had known sooner and was ready to soon tackle the role of fatherhood.

"I'm scared," Peter told Patricia and Em.

"Don't worry. We're coming up with a plan where you could initially have visitation rights with Samantha until your relationship with Teresa was more stable," Patricia said.

"I think Teresa and I have a stable relationship. I would hope she knows that I love her."

"She does know that," Em said.

"The question of your love for each other isn't really bothering me or the judge. It's the fact that Samantha needs a stable environment," Patricia added.

"What if we got married?" Peter asked.

"That would most likely help the case over time. Of course, you and Teresa would have to work that out before we could present it to the judge. Do you think you could maintain a marriage and forget all the hard details of the past?" Patricia wondered.

"Of course. I love her. It's that simple," Peter replied.

"Teresa wants to see you again real soon, Peter," Em added.

"Set up an appointment for me and Teresa. I need to visit her. I'd be happy to see her and tell her all the feelings that I have for her."

"Will do, Peter," Patricia said.

Peter told his parents the situation and they were surprisingly supportive of his willingness to give it another chance with Teresa and to try to be present in Samantha's life. When he mentioned the topic of marriage, however, they were a little concerned.

"This job isn't paying you a lot of money," Megan said.

"It doesn't matter," Peter stated.

"Of course, it matters, son!" Josh screamed.

"Samantha is my daughter. I can give her a life she deserves full of love and hope. Hope is something she needs in her life right now. I hope you can both understand that. Maybe Teresa and I could provide that for her."

"We just don't want to see you get hurt or Samantha have less than what she has now," Megan explained.

"She'll have a lot if I stick by Teresa and we're both there for Samantha," Peter explained.

"You're our son. We'll support you in whatever decision you make. It's just that Teresa has to calm down and live a normal life. Do you think she's capable of that?"

"Of course, Dad. She learned a lot. At least I'm almost certain she's learned from what Em has told me. I will speak to Teresa soon. And when I do, I'll consider everything before I make my final decision," Peter said.

As a little bit of time passed and Teresa's case was presented before the judge, it was decided that she did indeed act in self-defense. Teresa was going to be released from jail very soon. Patricia just had to discuss some things with her before she could be let go from the prison.

Patricia set up an appointment with Peter and Teresa in the jail. Patricia had Peter wait outside the visiting room while she prepared Teresa for Peter's visit.

"Hi, Teresa. I have Peter with me today and he is excited to see you. Are you excited to see him?"

"Yes, of course. You can let him in."

"Are you sure he's going to feel ok around you? Are you in a good enough mood to talk about your release?"

"Of course, I am. I can't wait to talk to him. Let him in."

When Peter was called in, he walked over to Teresa and saw that she had looked a lot less glamorous than he had remembered her, but he loved her so much. She had hit a low that he hoped he would never reach in his own life and was eager to build her confidence back up.

"Hi baby," Peter said as he sat across from Teresa who was behind a plastic barrier.

Peter placed his hand against the barrier as Teresa put her hand against it as well.

"How did we get here?" Teresa asked.

"Love. It's the only thing that could get us in so much trouble," Peter responded.

"Patricia said she's going to talk to me and wanted you to tell me what's going to happen when I get out of here. What's going to happen?"

"You'll stay with Em for a little while we work on our relationship and we'll tell Samantha one day in the not-too-distant future about us."

"What about us?"

"Well, about me. That I'm her father."

"Are you sure you can be there for her? You may leave us. That's what I'm scared of most."

"I won't leave you. Ever. I have nowhere else I want to go," Peter said as he smiled.

"I thought about us getting married one day," Teresa said.

"I'm actually thinking about it more than I think about anything else these days."

"Really?"

"Really. I am ready to get married and know what it's like to have a family. It's always been a dream of mine and I'm ready to make it come true."

"I can't wait. Are you going to propose?"

"I didn't get a ring, yet. But I will," Peter said as put his hand back on the plastic barrier and started to ask her to marry him.

"Will you, Teresa, take me to be your lawfully wedded husband?"

"Only if you'll have me as your wife, Peter," Teresa said as she started to cry with her hand up against the barrier as well.

Patricia was looking over and saw that things were going well. She was going to see if she could arrange Teresa's release as soon as possible. Patricia believed Teresa needed to get out of jail and begin her new life.

Chapter 57

When Teresa was let out of prison, Peter and Em were waiting for her. They all got in a cab that Peter paid for to take Teresa and Em to their home and Peter wanted to stay there with them for a little while. Peter wanted to see his daughter, Samantha, and realize the possibilities that awaited him in their new life together.

Andrea and God were looking down at the situation. Andrea was feeling very emotional as she felt tears coming on. God looked over to her.

"I see this working out much better than we could have hoped for," God said.

"I feel bad for all Teresa had to endure," Andrea stated.

"Suffering and desperation are part of the human condition but it's Peter who has impressed me much more than I thought he would. His willingness to accept Teresa for who she is, well, that's absolutely remarkable. He is loving someone completely and that's something John never truly had the opportunity to do in his life."

"Are you glad we sent him back then?"

"Well, it's not over yet. Let's make sure they get married."

"They will. At least, I hope they will."

"Let's see what happens," God stated.

Peter purchased an engagement ring for Teresa at a jewelry store at the local shopping mall. He felt excited giving it to her as soon as he picked it out as she was waiting across from the store on a bench to see what ring he would choose for her.

"When do you think I could move back in with you" Teresa asked Peter.

"Why?"

"I want to be with you. I've learned to stop feeling so depressed about what I don't have and to start cherishing the wonderful things I do have in my life."

"As soon as we get married. I think we can move back in together. That's what was decided. We can check with Em later."

"I can't wait for us to be back on our own and, one day, together with Samantha."

"It will probably happen sooner than we least expect."

As Peter started to go out with Teresa and Samantha on the weekends, he started to grow increasingly sad about not being there for his daughter's birth. Em provided him with pictures to look at which were so fascinating to Peter. He loved both Teresa and Samantha with all his heart but, at night, his dreams weren't as hopeful as they had been in the past. Peter would dream of failure and not having enough money to take his family out every weekend. He grew concerned and started to pray within himself.

Dear God

Please let me know things will be OK when I marry Teresa. I want to be able to provide for her and our daughter, Samantha. I need this more than anything I've ever asked for before. Please point me in the right direction and keep me safe and them safe. I need to be employed so I can provide for them, at least for a little while. I hope you know what I mean. Thanks for all you've done for me. I love them so much. Thanks, God, for giving me a family. It's all I ever wanted.

Chapter 58

Peter was going to marry Teresa at City Hall in three days. He was scared and hopeful, simultaneously, and constantly prayed for everything to go smoothly in the days leading up to the ceremony. He wanted Teresa's attacker to be kept in jail for a very long time and, from he was told, the guy wouldn't be released for quite a while.

Teresa planned on letting Samantha know that Peter was her true father. Teresa was very excited about letting her daughter know this fact. She just wanted to wait until she was officially married to Peter to reveal all the details to Samantha.

As Peter sat in his apartment the night before the wedding, he started to feel like everything that was happening was too good to be true. He feared that Teresa may cheat on him again and was also quite concerned that he wouldn't be able to raise Samantha to be a decent young woman.

Since Peter had a headache that evening, he decided to take some aspirin to see if it would help him feel better. Peter put his head down and wasn't sure what the future would hold for him. He needed answers and hoped that God would provide him with a sign that marrying Teresa was the right thing to do.

That night while he slept, he received a visit from God. He could clearly see that this vision of Him was as real as he ever could imagine. God began to speak to Peter.

I love you, Peter. I feel you have come a long way and the best way to show your faith in me is to marry Teresa and provide for her the best you can. Never feel like your best isn't good enough for it is. Marry her for me. It will prove your compassion and taking care of your daughter will prove that you are strong enough to love someone completely other than yourself. I know you loved your parents but now you're presented with a different kind of love to give. The kind of love that can change lives and continue to be passed down to future generations through your daughter or other children you may have. You are making the right decision. I promise you, son.

Peter hardly remembered the dream he had the night before when he woke up. He did however feel more secure and had more faith in himself than he previously did. Teresa was going to meet him with Samantha at City Hall. His parents were going to be there as well. Em was also going to be in attendance.

Peter boarded a downtown train to City Hall. He was dressed in a nice greyish suit with a striped tie and had flowers he had purchased at a local florist. These flowers were symbolic to him of his desire to create something beautiful with the family he was going to be a part of.

When he arrived at the location, there were four couples ahead of them as Teresa informed him. Samantha looked undoubtedly sweet wearing a cute, elegant, white dress. Peter's father hugged him tight.

"It's going to be good," Josh said.

"Thanks for coming guys," Peter said to his parents.

"We never would have missed it," Megan stated.

As they were waiting to be called, Peter held Teresa's hand so very tightly and looked into her eyes which seemed more innocent to him that they ever had before. It was time for a new beginning. This woman in front of Peter who he was about to marry hardly seemed like someone who had lived the past Teresa had actually lived. He loved her completely and was ready to take her future to a new level of happiness.

They kissed as they were pronounced husband and wife. Em and Peter's parents had planned a reception for them at a hall in Queens and invited some friends of the families to attend. It was a small celebration, but they were all together. When the moment came for Peter and Teresa to share their first dance, they were asked what their favorite song was.

"I'm not sure I have a favorite song," Teresa said.

"We have to come up with a song that's our song," Peter explained.

"I do have one that I used to love. It's really easy for me to remember. "Breakaway" by Kelly Clarkson. It was my absolute favorite when I was younger," Teresa said.

"I love that song," Peter responded.

"I figured you would," Teresa stated.

Em found the song on her iPhone and connected to the song to the speakers in the hall. As the song began to play, Peter and Teresa started to slow dance and Teresa put her head on his shoulder feeling safe from all harm and cherishing the moment she was in.

Towards the end of the song, Peter and Teresa kissed and Samantha started clapping her hands. Everybody else followed Samantha's example and applauded the new couple on their new marriage.

Chapter 59

On the evening of their wedding, Peter and Teresa spent the night together at Peter's apartment. They were trying to figure out when they could move in together permanently to begin their new life together. They needed to work out all the details soon so they could begin living their new life as a couple.

In a few weeks, it was decided that the time had come to tell Samantha that Peter was her biological father. Teresa didn't want to tell Samantha so soon but due to pressure from Peter and Patricia, as well as Em, she believed it was the right time.

At Em's home one Saturday afternoon, Peter showed up ready to tell Samantha the truth regarding her true parentage. Teresa let him in as Samantha was watching television on the couch. Teresa lowered the volume on the couch as she asked Em and her husband to go upstairs to give them some privacy.

"There's something we have to tell you, Samantha," Teresa said.

"What is it, Mommy?"

"Well, you know. Mommy and Peter are married now, and we wanted to talk to you about something. Something really important."

"That's right," Peter stated.

"We have something we need to let you know," Teresa explained.

"You know how your friends have a mother and a father?" Peter asked Samantha.

"Yeah," Samantha responded.

"Well, mommy and daddy want to let you in on a little secret," Peter said.

"What's the secret?" Samantha asked.

"Every child has two biological parents," Peter started to explain.

"She doesn't understand what biological means," Teresa said.

"Yes, I do, Mommy," said Samantha.

Peter asked her, "What's biological mean?"

"It means…I don't know."

"See, Samantha. We have to explain it to you," Peter continued.

Teresa asked Peter, "Do we have to tell her now?"

"Tell me what?" Samantha asked.

Peter decided to just let out the information they were so desperately trying to convey.

"We're your parents, I'm your father, and that's that. Do we want to go to the carnival in the park next weekend?"

"You're my Daddy?"

"Yes, Samantha, I am," Peter stated.

"OK. Let's go to the carnival."

"It's coming up soon but we're going to go," Peter explained.

"Can I hug you, Daddy?"

"Sure, Samantha."

Teresa smiled as everything seemed to be a lot easier than she thought it would be and Samantha accepted Peter as her father.

As the days passed, and Teresa found herself completely moved in with Peter, Teresa would apply for jobs as Peter worked during the day. She had worked on a new resume with a service that Patricia provided for her. Although there was not a lot of professional experience on the resume, it seemed well-written, and Teresa anxiously awaited getting a new job to pass the time until Samantha could come live with them. Since they would need a bigger apartment to take Samantha in, Teresa knew that dreams would take time to achieve.

Teresa found herself going into different stores and giving in her resume. She went to a 99 cents store and a yogurt store and handed her resume to the people working there.

At his job, Peter was going through the motions trying to make himself feel the company he was in valued him more than it did. He loved Teresa and knew she was looking for work. Peter wanted Teresa to raise Samantha and for all of three of them to live together. When he thought hard about the situation, however, he wanted to change his job but knew his medical insurance there was now covering

Teresa as well. Peter planned on adding Samantha to the insurance very soon which would take some extra disposable income away. He didn't mind but he wished there was more money to go around.

Back at their apartment, Teresa sat on the couch and closed her eyes. She started to think of what life would be like if Samantha was there. Teresa began thinking what it would be like to take her daughter to school and pick her up. Doing something simple like that would give her more of a sense of purpose. Em wanted to transfer Samantha to a school closer to where Peter and Teresa lived. It was just a matter of Em believing that Teresa was up to the challenge.

Teresa began to hate herself for the life she had lived in the past. She wasn't sure if she'd ever have to explain herself to her daughter one day, but Teresa was almost certain that questions would be asked regarding her past.

It felt weird to Teresa to not have to struggle for money and pay rent. Peter's salary was covering the bills and Teresa learned to accept that it was better for her to be safe than to be making money.

At about 3 in the afternoon, Teresa started crying. She had just gotten off the phone with Samantha who was at Em's house. Teresa wanted to go over and see her daughter but just felt hopeless in the moment. She was thinking that things would take too long to become the way she wanted them to be. She walked over to the medicine cabinet and took a couple of aspirin. She needed to be stronger and to feel better. She waited for Peter to come home so they could talk. A few hour later, Peter walked in.

"Hi, baby," Peter said.

"How was your day?"

"It was OK. I thought you'd call me in the afternoon, though,"

"I didn't want to disturb you at work,"

"That's understandable. But, you know, you can call me anytime. If I'm really busy, I'll just call you back."

"I don't know why but I was feeling like it's time to try to get Samantha to live with us."

"We'll need a bigger place for that," Peter stated.

"I was thinking. We could give her the bedroom and we could open up the couch and sleep on it instead."

"What about all our stuff in the room?"

"We can move it somewhere in the living room. Don't you think?"

"What's really bothering you?"

"Nobody's calling me for a job, so I'd prefer spending my free time with my daughter. That's all."

"That makes sense. Is everything OK with Patricia and Em if we do that?"

"I haven't asked them."

"I will ask them for you. Are you still going to therapy?"

"I went this week. I don't feel happy about myself going there. I know I have to but I'd much rather be with Samantha."

"I understand that. We'll have to see what possibilities we have. Then, we'll do something. OK, baby?"

Teresa took Peter's hand as they sat beside each other on the couch, and she started to kiss his lips feeling happy he was home. It seemed like it took so long for him to come home as the hours trickled by so slowly for her that day.

Chapter 60

Peter inquired about moving Samantha in with them. It didn't seem it was the right time being as Samantha had just started school. It was recommended that Peter work on trying to get an apartment with an extra room in the meantime.

Teresa felt like true happiness seemed so far away but was content being with Peter. She enjoyed his company and she believed he valued her more than other men she had known in the past.

When Peter was working one Wednesday morning, Teresa was feeling deeply depressed. Although she hadn't felt bad until recently, she needed to see her daughter. She took a train to Samantha's school and asked the principal to see her.

"Is it an emergency?" the principal asked.

"Yes, yes, it is," Teresa responded.

"What's going on?"

"One of my friends just passed away."

"Oh, no. I don't think it's good to pull Samantha out of class to tell her that kind of news. Where's your sister? It seems she's the only one on the emergency card that can take her from school."

"Right. I guess I can deal with it on my own."

"If your sister calls us then we can release Samantha."

"OK. I'll see what Em says. Thanks anyway."

Teresa walked away feeling hopeless. She couldn't even see her own daughter. She dialed Peter's phone number but before it started ringing, she hung up. She didn't want to bother Peter at work. She went back home and took a bottle of pills from the medicine cabinet. Teresa started taking a few of the pain relief pills. Then, she slowly started to take one more and one by one, she started swallowing them. Then, her eyes closed as she felt her body shaking.

Teresa saw a tunnel with a bright, white light at the end of it. She felt as if her body was traveling through the tunnel. When she reached the end of it, the light turned red, and she began to see fire. She was scared. Feeling things far beyond the physical, Teresa asked, "Where am I?"

"Where do you want to be?" a very loud and distinct voice asked her.

"I'm scared," Teresa responded.

"What do you want to do? Do you wish to end your life?"

"I'm scared. I don't know what I want to do."

"Decide now. Your body is trembling on Earth. Do you wish to join me in Hell or live on Earth the remainder of your living days?"

"Who are you?"

"I'm the one who takes souls who commit suicide."

"The devil?"

"I go by many names. Decide in five seconds or you will be mine."

"I want to live!" she screamed as the tunnel took her back in reverse and she was in her body again.

She opened her eyes and started spitting up and throwing up the pills she had taken. She was sitting on the bathroom floor covered with vomit as she took a towel and cleaned herself up. It was still several hours before Peter would be home from work. Teresa took a shower. She wanted to call for help but realized the only person who could truly help her was herself. There was nobody else to call. There was only one person who could make the difference that needed to be made. It was only Teresa, herself, who could change her own life.

Scared that she had almost killed herself, she sat down on the couch and put on television. She was temporarily feeling better as she realized she needed to do more if she wanted a job. She needed to cherish her life and tell Peter how much she appreciated him. She felt a newfound joy and couldn't wait to do what she had to do to win back Samantha into her life. Then, the phone rang.

"Hello, Teresa?"

"Hi, Em."

"Who died? The school told me you were looking to see Samantha. Was it someone we knew?"

"Just someone I knew. I just wanted to see Samantha so I could feel a little better about it."

"Do you want us to come and see you? Are you home?"

"Yes, I'm home. I'd love for you two to come here and see me. I'm feeling really lonely."

"Who was this person who died?"

"Just a person I used to know. I hardly knew her. I'm not going to the funeral. I just felt bad when I heard the news."

"I see. We'll be right over," Em said.

Teresa realized she was speaking about herself when she said that the person she "hardly knew" had died. She was ready to get to know her true self again and was eagerly awaiting seeing her family for she knew that she could begin her life again with their support.

Chapter 61

Andrea and God were talking about some new cases when Andrea brought up the topic of "Peter."

"I see Peter made good on everything. He's married, he going to be taking his daughter in soon and is loving and supportive of Teresa," God stated.

"John never got to have the opportunities Peter will have for happiness," Andrea responded.

"John was a good man, but he was misguided. With Peter's support, Teresa will become a better woman and mother."

"Samantha deserves that."

"I know that when a person tries to take their own life and meets the devil, and then chooses life again that that person can find a new path on Earth in time to save their soul when they do truly die."

"Teresa has learned a lot. Let's see where her life takes her."

"I can only hope it takes her places she's never been before. All good places," God stated.

"Maybe Peter's life was meant to help her see something much more glorious than the life she found herself living," Andrea said.

"Well, we'll keep an eye on them. Let's move on to the other cases now. You have some people to greet coming up soon."

"Yes, I do. I'll start putting their files together."

Back on Earth, Peter started seeing changes in Teresa. Teresa was home with him one evening when she put her arms around him.

"I want to go to the beach," Teresa said.

"Well, it is the season," Peter responded.

"I think it's a great idea to take Em, Samantha and just go. It's something I've always wanted to do."

"There's no more time for hesitation. It's time to start living our lives and doing what we want to do to be happy."

"Happiness is what's it's all about. That's why I'm going to take charge with my resumes and start going out to these places in person. I'm not sending resumes out anymore that go into thin air. I'm going to make my presence known so I can get a good job."

"I may have to follow your lead. This job has some good benefits but I'm open to seeing if there's better out there. Really open to seeing if there's better out there for us, actually."

"There is better. We just have to open our eyes," Teresa said.

Chapter 62

Em, Peter, Teresa and Samantha took a train together to go to the beach one weekday afternoon. Peter had used a vacation day to spend time with his family. Peter had been saving money and was going to be getting a bigger apartment so Samantha could come live with him and Teresa. It was just a matter of a few more months.

When Peter was sitting alone on a beach towel as Samantha, Teresa and Em made their way out to the water, he closed his eyes. He envisioned the bright, sunny scenery that he had just witnessed as proof there was a Heaven on Earth. He spoke to himself and gave thanks to God.

Thank you, God for giving me this chance to have a family and be happy. I know I had many chances in life and messed up so many times. I have no idea why I couldn't get it right before, but I feel I have it right now. Watch over me and my family and guide us in the right direction. Keep us safe from evil and point us straight towards happiness. Always.

Peter opened his eyes and saw the sun seemingly shining as brightly as it ever had before. Teresa lifted Samantha up in the air for a picture Em was about to take. They called Peter over to take a photo with them. Peter felt he had been living for a long time but now he was ready to truly live the way he was supposed to. He ran to his family and hoped everything would be fine one day. He held on for just a little while longer. He believed that "perfect" would come one day. Peter held his wife and kissed her on the beach while Samantha and Em playfully chased each other while running on the sand. He then knew one thing for certain. Perfect was here.